THE UNDERWEAR DARE

Lisa Nardini
&
Gina Nardini

Illustrated by:
Gina Christoffel

Sorelle Publishing Inc.

LCCN: 2011902739

ISBN: 0615435106
ISBN-13: 978-0615435107

For Bruce Coville and his four golden words.

ACKNOWLEDGMENTS

The Nardini Sisters would like to thank their families for their continuing support, especially their Mom, sister Sucia, nephew, Josh and niece, Marina. Much thanks to our editor, Diane Hollingsworth. We would also like to thank SCBWI (Society of Childrens Book Writers and Illustrators) and SCWG (Space Coast Writers' Guild) for all the knowledge gained though conferences we have attended and critiques we have received.

Gina would like to thank her husband, Scott and her friends who have provided support. Gina would also like to thank all her students who have provided an endless supply of childlike dialogue and wonder. Thanks guys!

Lisa would like to thank all her friends, especially Renae who has read everything she's ever written. Many thanks to the Delta flight attendants who have shown interest in her writing. Lisa would also like to thank her Monday night Childrens Writing Club for all their encouragement. A special thanks to Joe Riccardi and his keen eye for detail. And to Dean…who's riding on her coat tails.

CHAPTER 1

"Josh Miller, I'm gonna get you!"

I didn't have to turn around to know whose voice that was. Eddie was a legend at our school, plus he'd been yelling that particular phrase at me since kindergarten. I thought once we started fifth grade, he'd be tired of picking on me. Not so! If there was ever a record for longest time span for a bully, Eddie would be the champion.

"Hey, Josh. I'm right behind you." Eddie huffed and puffed between words.

I was short for my age, even though I had grown two inches over the summer. Eddie was gigantic. He was taller than most of our teachers and he was also pretty wide due to his love of cookies and fruity drinks. Even so, Eddie's size didn't slow down his speed. He was fast, but I was faster as I sprinted from the bus stop through our neighborhood.

I picked up the pace. I pumped my legs as fast as I could. It didn't help that my backpack was loaded down with library books. Hardbacks. I told Ms. Bullard, the Media Specialist, I preferred paperbacks, but she just laughed.

Small beads of sweat slid down my face. I tasted one, very salty. I heard Eddie's footsteps slow down and I knew he was tired. He was running out of steam. I didn't stop. I still had to pass three more houses before I was safely at my doorstep. Piece of cake!

"You're a dead man!" Eddie yelled. He was doubled over holding his side.

I slowed down a little, but not much. It could be a trick. I'd been fooled before, plus I only had two houses left.

Dang, just when I thought I was safe I saw old Miss Jenkins walking her French poodle, Gigi. Gigi had one of those poofy, silly, poodle cuts and pink toenail polish. Miss Jenkins was very talkative and never, ever, fastened Gigi's collar properly. Plus, they both wore too much perfume.

"Good afternoon, Josh. Why are you in such a hurry?" Miss Jenkins asked as she blocked the straight shot I had to my house.

I had no choice but to stop. Gigi worked her way out of the collar and ran around in circles excited to see me. I bent over to pat her head and she took off down the street. Luckily, there were no cars driving by. But no Eddie either. *Where did he go?*

"Oh my! Gigi! Stop, stop right now! I don't know how she gets out of that collar. Josh, can you please…?"

I threw down my backpack and sprinted to catch her before Miss Jenkins could finish her sentence. I scooped Gigi up just in time to save her from a truck that came flying around the corner.

Miss Jenkins was overjoyed with relief, "Thank you so much, Josh. I don't know why that keeps happening."

"Maybe you should tighten her collar a few notches," I suggested as I scanned the area for Eddie.

"Oh, I couldn't do that," Miss Jenkins said. "Gigi doesn't like anything tight around her neck. Do you baby?" she cooed to Gigi.

I was about to ask her how she knew this, but I didn't want to be rude. Instead I told her I had lots of homework to do and better get started. I ran at full speed to my front door and dug in my backpack for my house key. After removing four hardback books, I realized my key was gone. It had to be Eddie!

I knocked furiously on the door and rang the bell several times. From inside my house, Eddie pulled back the front window curtain and waved.

"Let me in, now! This isn't funny!" I yelled and knocked on the door again.

"Who is it?" Eddie asked, purposely making his voice sound like a girl.

"Come on Eddie," I pleaded.

"There's nobody here named Eddie," he mocked again in that high voice.

I was way ahead of him today. I had left the garage door opener hidden in the bushes for such emergencies. I sprinted to the bushes, retrieved the opener and presto! I was in the garage. I yanked on the door leading into the house. It was locked. I banged with all my might.

"Yes, who is it?" Eddie asked on the other side of the door. "It's a good thing I locked this door so no robbers could get in."

"Come on, Eddie. You win, let me in." I pleaded.

"There is no one here by that name," he said and snickered.

"Fine! Oh, Great and Strong Ruler who is 'Master of all in the Fifth Grade Realm', please let me in," I quoted.

"Who goes before the Master?" Eddie answered in a low booming voice.

"It is I, your humble servant Josh, who in no way can defeat the Great and Strong Master," I answered.

"Because why?" he bellowed.

"Because I am much too puny," I finished completely humiliated.

The locked clicked open and Eddie stood there laughing, "Someday I gotta record that on my phone."

Eddie wiggled the remote control in his hands as if it were a prize. Of course, that meant he had complete control over the big TV until his mom got home, or my dad got off early. Yes, that's right, my dad married Eddie's mom and now he's my stepbrother! This was definitely the worst year of my life. Thing is, I really liked Eddie's mom, Allie. She was nice, nothing at all like Eddie.

My mom died when I was really young and I don't remember much about her. But as much as I liked having a cool step-mom, the price of the step-brother was too high!

I walked into the living room and was instantly assaulted by a horrible smell.

Eddie laughed and said, "Silent but deadly, for your smelling pleasure!"

"Nasty fart." I said but he just laughed again. It smelled like boiled broccoli.

"Found this on the playground," Eddie said as he tossed me my house key.

"Yeah, if the playground is in my backpack," I mumbled.

"That's funny and true," Eddie said and turned his attention to the TV. He was watching some pirate show on the History Channel. And not a good one like Pirates of the Caribbean, but a show that explained what it was like to be a real pirate. Boring. I sat at the table and began doing my homework.

"Aren't you gonna do your homework?" I asked.

"Got it covered," he said.

When Eddie said, "Got it covered" it meant some poor kid was doing it for him. Eddie walked to the kitchen to get a soda. On the way back he released another "Silent but deadly" right next to me.

"Dang it, Eddie," I said and covered my nose. "I'm trying to do my homework."

"There is no safe place to hide from the Master!"

And that was the truth. There was no safe place to hide from Eddie. It wasn't fair that we had to share a bedroom. The only time I got a break from Eddie was when he visited his father every other weekend. And half the time his dad backed out with some lame excuse. I wanted him to move in with his dad permanently but my dad said that wasn't going to happen because he would have to change schools. For me, no Eddie at home or at school would be perfect. If I had my own room, then I would have a safe retreat. But that was just wishful thinking.

CHAPTER 2

Later that evening in our room, I slid into the bottom bunk bed while Eddie climbed the narrow ladder to the top bunk. I was mesmerized by how huge Eddie's feet were. They were almost as wide as they were long. They were very flat with no arches. Just looking at them made me think of caveman's feet. I couldn't help but laugh out loud.

"What's so funny, shrimp?" Eddie asked, as he flopped down on the mattress.

When his bed bowed above my head, I stopped laughing. A horrible vision of Eddie and the mattress falling on top of me during the night entered my mind. What a terrible way to die.

"I said, what's so funny, peewee?"

"Nothing." I wished I could come up with names to hurt him, but I couldn't think that fast on my feet. Oh, wait. I should have called him caveman. Darn. I reached over and turned off the light. The room went pitch black, just the way I liked it.

"Hey, turn on the nightlight. I can't sleep in total darkness," Eddie said nervously.

I flicked on the nightlight and laughed again. Big Eddie was afraid of the dark. *I bet all the kids at school would think that was hilarious*, I thought to myself.

As if reading my mind, Eddie said, "If you so much as tell anyone I'm, I'm...anyway I will pound you so hard your dad won't recognize you."

I stopped laughing. Eddie could probably do it to.

My dad knocked on the door and peeked inside. He flipped the light back on. "Boys? I know you're not asleep yet."

"Yeah, Dad?"

"Yeah, Jack?" Eddie said.

"Allie and I just had a long talk and we decided to give you each your own room," he announced.

"But Dad, we only have two rooms. Where will you and Allie sleep?" I asked.

"No, no. In the attic," my dad said and laughed.

"You and Mom are gonna sleep in the attic? Cool! I didn't even know there was one," Eddie exclaimed.

"No, Eddie," my dad explained. "Not us. We are going to convert the attic into a bedroom for one of you."

"I think I should get it because this was my house first," I said.

"I should get it. This was your room first, you should have it back," Eddie countered.

"No way," I replied. The attic was huge. I really wanted that room. It would be like living in a mansion.

Eddie yelled at me, "So, I had to leave my house and come live here with you."

My dad interrupted, "Hold it. Whoa! Allie and I have already decided who gets the room."

Eddie and I both shut up. It was so quiet you could hear the music playing downstairs. Allie played music almost every night. At first, I didn't like it but now I was getting used to it. It was opera. Allie told me that opera calmed her down and kept her in a good mood.

Not being able to take the silence anymore, Eddie caved in, "So Jack, who did you choose?"

"We've decided it's up to you," he answered.

"Me!" Eddie yelled. "Great, I choose me."

My dad quickly said, "No, not you!"

"Me?" I screamed. "Alright, this is the best news ever!"

"No, not you either," Dad said.

"I don't get it," Eddie said and for once I agreed with him.

My dad explained. "Allie and I know this hasn't been an easy adjustment for either of you. Our marriage happened fast, and I know there's been tension between you two for a long time."

"Try kindergarten," I mumbled.

Eddie leaned over the bunk bed and mouthed to me, "You're dead."

"Boys, focus. There's only one fair way to settle a decision this big. So we are leaving it up to the two of you to figure out who gets the attic. Construction starts next week. That leaves a month to decide. Oh, and there better not be any fighting or arguing about it. Got it?"

"Yes, Dad," I said.

"Eddie?" Jack asked.

"Um, no fighting."

"Okay, 'night boys," he turned off the light and closed the door.

"Hey, Eddie," I whispered. "We can settle this right now. I have $17.31. It's all yours if you give me the room."

Eddie laughed. "I've got more than that in the front pocket of the jeans I just took off."

"Seriously?" I asked.

"I had a very profitable week at school."

"Doing what?" I inquired.

"Getting paid for protecting classmates."

"Protecting them from who?" I couldn't wait to hear his answer.

"From me, of course. It's a new thing I started this year."

"Our classmates pay you to protect them from you?" I couldn't believe it.

"It's very lucrative," Eddie laughed. "So, how much do you want for the room?"

"No way, I'm not for sale."

"What if I told you I would give you three figures worth?" Eddie said.

"No." I stood my ground.

"How about four figures?" Eddie bargained.

"You have four?" I knew that was at least one thousand dollars.

"Um, no. But I do have three," Eddie admitted.

"What if I give you all my video games?" I asked.

"Your video games stink. Mine are way better." Eddie countered.

I couldn't argue with that. It was true. Eddie had a better collection. "How about all my DVD's?" I offered. Silence from Eddie. I tried again. "Final offer, all my money, my video games and all my DVD's."

Eddie spoke up, "You have less money than me. Your video games stink. Your DVD's stink even more."

"Wait, I wasn't finished. All that, plus I will do your homework for a week," I added.

"How about a month?"

"Deal!" I said.

"No, just kidding," Eddie teased.

"Loser," I said under my breath.

"What?"

I quickly came up with more bargaining items. "What if I throw in my skateboard and dirt bike?"

"Your skateboard is too girlie for me and the dirt bike is too small," Eddie said.

"What do you mean my skateboard's too girlie?"

"It has a hot pink swirl on it."

"Hey, your Mom bought it for me!"

"I know. I told her your favorite color was pink."

"You are such a jerk!"

Eddie jumped down from the top bunk in one swift motion and pulled me to the floor. "No, you're the jerk! Come on, you little wiener."

"Hey, Dad said no fighting," I yelled hoping my dad would hear.

"What are you going to do, snitch on me?"

Through the headlock I mumbled, "Yeah."

Eddie released me from the headlock and pinned me to the ground. "Fine, I won't fight. You couldn't win anyway." Instead, Eddie threw his head back and started gulping air.

I knew what was coming. Eddie was legendary for it. If he didn't fight you, this was his back-up move. Some say it was worse than being hit.

"No, no!" I cried as I tried to turn my head away from Eddie. I took a quick breath and held it in.

"You have to breathe sometime." Eddie tormented me.

My face was turning red. I knew I would have to breathe soon. No longer able to hold it in, I let out my breath.

Eddie leaned in close, real close. "Buuurrrp!"

It was the loudest burp I had ever heard. And the smelliest! I didn't mean to smell it but I had to breathe. "Agh! It's in my mouth!" I could practically taste the spaghetti and meatballs we had for dinner a couple of hours ago. Oh, no! Another one was coming.

"Buuurrrp!"

I almost threw up in my mouth. Garlic bread! I could taste and smell the garlic bread on that last burp. I told Dad there was too much garlic on the bread, but Dad said you could never have enough garlic. Boy, was he wrong! Eddie let go of me and crawled back up to his bed.

With my ears still ringing from the vibrato of Eddie's burps, I stumbled into the lower bunk. "You're disgusting," I spat.

"You're just jealous 'cause you can't do it."

Deep down I knew that Eddie was right. I could only burp if I drank lemon-lime soda really fast. Even then, my burps weren't on the same Richter Scale as Eddie's. I longed to ask Eddie his secret, but knew a true master would never reveal it.

"Hey, remember that time when Marina Ashton was giving that report and I..." Eddie was laughing so hard he couldn't finish his sentence.

Did I ever! It was at the beginning of the year. Marina was giving her report on horses and she asked if anyone had any questions. Eddie raised his hand. The whole class grew quiet, because Eddie never participated in class unless he had to. He gulped air and burped really loud. Everyone laughed and Marina got mad and so did Ms. Waverly. Ms. Waverly asked what his question was and Eddie replied, "What did I have for lunch?" The whole classroom lost it again. Eddie was sent to the principal's office.

"That was great. Except that you got in trouble," I said.

"For once, I'd like to see you get into trouble," Eddie said.

"For once, I'd like to see you *not* get into trouble. I bet you couldn't go a whole day without bullying someone or taking their money," I replied snidely.

"I could too, easily. I could go a whole week."

It was times like this that my straight-A, honor roll brain jumped into overdrive. I knew there was only one way to beat Eddie and that was to play by his rules, which unfortunately were always dirty. The plan that formed in my mind was not a nice one. "What if the person who completes the craziest dare at school gets the attic room?"

Eddie was speechless. We were both engrossed in our own thoughts. Eddie finally broke the silence. "I dare you to burp really loud in class," he challenged.

I was afraid Eddie would come up with something like that. "Yeah, okay. I can do that. But then I dare you to stop being a bully for one whole week."

Eddie let out a sigh of relief. "Easy."

"And you have to be nice to everyone you have ever been mean to."

"How am I supposed to do that? It would take forever!" Eddie whined.

"True. But I'm giving you a week." I said.

"Fine. But your burp can't be a regular burp. It has to be loud enough for everyone to hear including Ms. Waverly. And it has to be at a time when no one expects it. Can you do it?"

Not wanting to appear unsure, I said, "No problem. Do I get the whole week too?"

"Yeah. We will start on Monday. Whoever doesn't complete his dare by Friday loses. Agreed?" Eddie asked.

"Agreed. Wait!"

Eddie laughed. "Are you backing out already?"

"No. But what happens if we both complete our dares? Then who gets the room?" I asked.

"I didn't think of that," Eddie said.

"I know. We'll have back-up dares for the next week," I said.

"Genius," Eddie replied.

The next week was poetry week. I knew there was some kind of great dare in there, but couldn't figure it out. Eddie, on the other hand, didn't have a problem with coming up with my next dare.

"You have to fart really loud in class. And in front of Ms. Waverly. And it has to smell, too." Eddie laughed.

Dang, Eddie was picking all the things that he was good at. He was also a legend when it came to farting. There was this one time, in science class, when Eddie farted too close to the sulfur beaker and it exploded. The whole class had to evacuate. He got sent to the principal's office for that one too.

"Well, what about me? Can't think of anything?" Eddie inquired.

And just then it hit me, "You know how we have our poetry unit in two weeks?"

"Yeah," Eddie said cautiously.

"You have to write a love poem to Ms. Waverly and recite in front of the class," I said.

"No way. Ms. Waverly is so old and ugly."

"Can't do it?" I smirked.

"You little...I can do it. Wait! What if we both do our dares again, who wins?"

"If we both do our dares, then the third week should be a shared dare. One so bad that whoever does it first, automatically wins hands down."

"I like the sound of that," Eddie said.

"You would. Hey, we have to make a pact. If either one of us tells anybody about these dares, especially our parents, then he automatically loses. Agreed?"

"Agreed," Eddie jumped down to face me. "I got it. The final dare. The ultimate dare!"

"What?" I asked.

"Whoever runs though the cafetorium in his underwear during lunchtime wins!"

"Are you crazy? Do you know how much trouble we could get into?" I asked.

"Are you in?" Eddie narrowed his eyes.

"I'm in," I said reluctantly. I didn't sleep well the rest of the night.

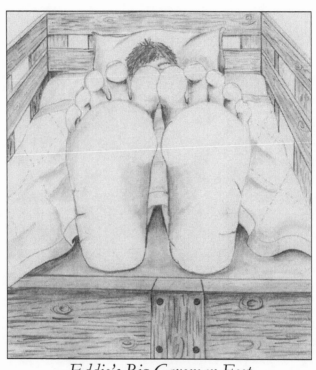

Eddie's Big Caveman Feet

CHAPTER 3

Even though it was Saturday and I got to sleep in, I was cranky and tired. I tossed and turned all night and wondered what I'd gotten myself into. Eddie, on the other hand, slept like a baby. His snores echoed off the walls and burrowed into my ears. He really was the king of disgusting sounds.

I knew I had to prepare myself for the coming week if I was going to succeed. I made a few notes before getting dressed and then headed downstairs. Allie was already up. The rich smell of bacon filled the room and not just regular bacon but the thick, smoky kind.

"Do you want some bacon and eggs?" Allie asked cheerfully as she tucked a strand of long brown hair back into the messy bun from which it had escaped.

"I'll have some bacon, but eggs give me gas, maybe next Monday," I said.

Allie looked puzzled as I filled a cereal bowl.

"I'm going to the store later, do you want anything special for your lunch this week?" she asked.

"Actually, yes. I've made a list." I pulled it out of my back pocket and handed it to her.

"Pop-rocks, lemon-lime soda and straws. I can't get you these things; they'll rot your teeth and give you indigestion."

"Exactly."

"What?"

"I mean it's for a science project about food that gives you indigestion," I quickly answered.

"Oh, alright," she said not thoroughly convinced.

Eddie's caveman feet pounded down the stairs. *Is he ever quiet?* I thought.

*　　　*　　　*

On Monday morning, the yellow school bus doors folded open with a hiss. Eddie stomped aboard and I followed behind him. The noisy bus grew instantly quiet as Eddie made his way down the aisle. I knew Eddie would never be able to be nice to everyone he wronged. The attic room was as good as mine.

Eddie passed Matthew, a somewhat geeky boy in our class. Matthew opened his lunch box and removed his daily offering. It was an enormous snicker-doodle cookie. The smell of cinnamon and sugar made Eddie's stomach rumble loud enough for me to hear.

"My mom just made these this morning," Matthew said nervously.

I peeked around Eddie's shoulder. "Yum, delicious," I said as I tried to goad Eddie into taking the cookie. "I bet you wish you had a tall glass of cold milk right now. Huh, Eddie?"

"That does sound good," Eddie agreed and grabbed the cookie. "Wait a minute..." he said as he caught onto my scheme and tossed the cookie back into Matthew's lunch box.

"Nice try, shrimp boy," Eddie said to me.

Matthew looked confused as Eddie continued down the aisle.

Bria, a shy girl with blonde hair and chubby cheeks, held out a folder for Eddie.

"Here's the book report you asked for," she said.

"Did you make it a C-, because last time the B+ made Ms. Waverly suspicious," he growled.

"Yes and I even spilled some jelly on it to make it more authentic," Bria said.

"I don't know what that means, but that word better not be in the report," Eddie added.

"Authentic means its real, as in it really looks like you wrote it," Bria said.

Eddie's face fell as he realized his error. He couldn't take the report or he would lose the bet.

"Keep it, Bria. Maybe you can rewrite it and use it yourself," Eddie said.

"Okay," Bria answered with a puzzled look.

As Eddie continued down the aisle, several students on the bus held up a dollar bill for him to collect. I guess I never noticed that before because I usually sit in the front as far away from Eddie as possible. But for this week, I wanted to keep my eye on him.

"Here's this week's protection money," one freckled-face boy said as he handed Eddie a dollar.

"That's impressive," I said to Eddie. "No wonder you have such a good DVD collection."

"I won't be collecting protection money this week," Eddie announced in a loud voice.

The freckled face boy started crying. "Does that mean we won't be protected from you?"

"No," he continued, "I'm taking the week off, but I will collect next week and the price will be double."

I nudged Eddie in the ribs, "Thanks for the room," I whispered in his ear.

Eddie wasn't going to let me win that fast, so he quickly said, "What I meant to say was next week is free, too."

Cheers all around the bus. I couldn't believe they actually cheered for Eddie. Eddie smiled and raised his hands in victory. He loved the attention. You'd have thought he'd just become the President of the United States. This wasn't working at all like I planned.

*   *   *

I sat in the cafetorium and opened my lunch box. I tossed a handful of pop-rocks in my mouth. It felt like a small firework display exploding against my checks. I sipped the lemon-lime soda through a straw. My nose tickled at the combination of fizzy soda and pop-rocks but I managed to keep it down.

Paul, a tall, blonde boy, laughed exposing pieces of his bologna sandwich in his mouth. "I can't believe you just did that! Nobody mixes those two things. You could die!"

"That's a stupid rumor," Chelsea, a pretty girl with brown skin said.

"No, it's true," a short boy named Manny said. "It happened to my cousin's best-friend's brother. His head blew off."

"I do feel a little queasy," I said.

"Serves you right for eating that way." Marina, the smartest girl in the class said as she drank her milk.

I continued drinking my soda.

"Idiot," Marina said under her breath.

I looked over at Eddie eating lunch by himself. Every once in a while a kid would walk over and offer him a tasty treat. I saw Eddie turned down two Snickers bars, a bag of potato chips, a chocolate pudding, a juice box, and a strawberry cupcake. Eddie was taking this more seriously than I ever imagined. I doubled my efforts to finish the lemon-lime soda. My stomach gurgled loudly.

"Are you alright?" Chelsea asked.

"He's going to blow, just like my cousin's best-friend's brother!" Manny yelled.

I put my hand over my mouth and ran for the bathroom.

"Stupid boys," Marina said as she daintily dipped a chicken nugget into honey-mustard sauce.

*   *   *

The porcelain sink felt cool under my fingers as I stared at myself in the mirror. My skin was the same green color as the lemon-lime soda can. My sandy-brown hair stood up in different angles and my brown eyes were bloodshot. I felt pressure building up in my throat. Just then, Eddie barged through the door.

"I just heard a rumor that your head blew off," he said. "I thought I'd come see for myself. You look okay to me for a green dude," he said as he slapped me on the back.

"Burrrrp!" It came out of my mouth before I knew it and it was my best burp ever.

"I did it!"

"Too bad no one heard it but me. It doesn't count," Eddie said.

"Wait, I feel another one coming on," I said and ran back into the cafetorium with Eddie on my heels. "This one will count," I said as I opened my mouth. But instead of burping, a spew of vomit erupted from my lips. It hit the floor with a splat as the entire student body moaned in disgust.

Eddie and I stared at the vomit in amazement as little pop-rocks continued to burst in the gooey mess.

"Cool, popping vomit," Eddie exclaimed.

*　　　*　　　*

I hated the school clinic. The bed was rock hard and every time I moved, the sanitary paper crinkled beneath me. Nurse Turley leaned over me and her breath smelled like tuna fish. She put her hand on my forehead.

"You don't feel hot," she said. "Maybe it was something you ate. What did you have for lunch?"

"The usual," I answered not wanting to give myself away.

"And what was the usual?" she asked.

I had to think fast. I knew I couldn't say pop-rocks and lemon-lime soda.

"Fruit," I answered.

"What kind of fruit?"

"Mostly lemons and limes," I said.

"That's your usual lunch?"

I remembered the pop-rocks were grape-flavored. "I also had some grapes," I added.

"Are you familiar with the food pyramid?" she questioned. She pointed to a poster of the food pyramid on the wall. It was next to a poster that showed kids covered with disgusting rashes and chicken pox.

I felt the bile rise in my throat as I stared at the gross disease poster. "I don't feel so good."

"Of course you don't. You have too much acid in your stomach from all that fruit. I'll give you a sip of carbonated soda to settle your stomach. Would you like grape or lemon-lime?" she asked.

"Neither," I moaned.

"Either? Okay, lemon-lime coming right up," she said cheerfully. She handed me a small Dixie Cup of soda. The red polka-dots on the Dixie Cup looked just like the chicken pox on the poster.

"Drink up," she ordered.

As I drank the soda, I couldn't help but stare at the poster. It showed a kid's arm covered in red splotches with the word **Rubella** written under it. *What's Rubella? Gross!* I thought. It was all too much. Poor Nurse Turley didn't stand a chance. Bull's eye! My vomit hit her squarely in the chest. Now I understood why she always wore a smock. I rolled over and closed my eyes. This really wasn't going at all like I planned.

CHAPTER 4

The damp washcloth felt cool on my forehead. I snuggled deeper into the couch and pulled the quilt up to my chin. I wasn't really sick, but I liked how Allie doted on me. My stomach felt fine now that I ate some chicken soup. Mostly, I just liked having a mom.

"Feeling better?" Allie asked as she entered the room. She placed a hand on my cheek.

"Yeah, much,"

"Nurse Turley said something interesting when I picked you up from school," she said.

"Really? What?" I said nervously. Maybe Allie was onto me.

"She said something about you eating only lemons and limes for lunch."

I knew I was the worst liar in the world. If only I had Eddie's skill in that department.

"Yeah, that's right, he did." Eddie said as he swaggered through the door and tossed his backpack on the floor. "It was awesome!"

"Hi sweetie," Allie said to Eddie. "How was your day?"

"Josh set a new puking record at school, so I'd say pretty great," Eddie answered.

"Why would you eat lemons and limes for lunch?" she asked me again.

"And grapes. Didn't you eat some grapes, or something grape flavored?" Eddie added with a mischievous grin.

"Grapes, lemons and limes? That's a lot of acid for one meal. Why did you do it, it wasn't a dare was it?" Allie asked.

How did she know? I thought. "Well, it was like this, you see, um, it, ah…" I was going down in flames and then something amazing happened. Eddie, the master liar, came to my rescue.

"See Mom, Josh and I were watching this show last week about the lives of real pirates and we were all sitting together at lunch today talking about how the pirates got scurvy, and…"

"Wait," Allie interrupted.

Oh great, I thought, the one time Eddie's lie didn't work.

"You mean to tell me you and Josh sit together at lunch?" she said and looked surprised.

"Sure, we do. Anyway, we were talking about the ocean voyages of pirates and how they always keep citrus on board to prevent scurvy. Then Josh was worried he might have scurvy because he hadn't eaten any fruit in a while. So, I raided the teachers' ice tea table when no one was looking and gave him the lemons and the limes to eat."

Eddie was a true genius! I looked at him in amazement. Eddie fired off a quick wink and a half grin. I could barely hold in my laughter. Eddie, big mean Eddie, just came up with a world class excuse and put himself in the line of fire to pull it off just to save my skin!

"I don't like you raiding the teachers' table," Allie said. "And if I hear of it again, you'll be in more trouble than you can imagine. But I'm glad to hear you boys are sitting together at lunch." she said and she patted both our heads and disappeared into the kitchen.

"That was priceless! You truly are the master. How did you remember all that stuff about pirates?" I asked.

"I always remember what I watch on TV," Eddie answered and you could tell he was quite pleased with himself.

That was true. Eddie always remembered everything he saw on TV. I realized this meant something important, but couldn't quite figure out what.

*   *   *

The next day, I was focused on the task at hand. I knew the pop rocks had been the fatal error. If I could bring myself to just drink the soda, I could pull it off. To make sure I burped in class, I came up with a clever plan. Tucked into the left leg pocket of my cargo pants were ten straws. A can of soda was in the right leg pocket.

As the entire class sat through Ms. Waverly's math lesson, I put my plan into action. My palms were sweaty from nerves, so I had to keep wiping them on my pants. But I knew I could pull it off.

"When adding fractions, how do you change the denominator and numerator?" Ms. Waverly droned. Marina's hand flew up. She knew everything.

My hand moved slowly down toward my left pant leg as I very carefully unzipped the zipper. It took me three full minutes to remove each straw and place them into my desk.

"Josh," Ms. Waverly said.

I snapped to attention. Ms. Waverly looked suspicious.

"Are you paying attention?" she asked.

"Yes," *How do they always know?*

"Then perhaps you should come up to the board and finish this problem," she said.

I walked up to the white board and stared. I grabbed the blue Expo Marker and effortlessly solved the problem of converting the denominator to a like number for both fractions and then added and reduced and was done. I only wished I could burp as easily as I could add fractions. I saw Eddie watching me. He looked impressed.

Ms. Waverly said thank you, but looked a little disappointed. She lived to catch kids not paying attention.

"We will spend the remainder of math block working on a fractions worksheet," she announced and began passing out the worksheets.

Whenever a teacher says "we will spend…" that really means us kids will spend…

Ms. Waverly sat down at her desk and began grading papers. I started assembling my straws secretly inside my desk. Manny's desk was right next to mine and he watched me with a baffled expression on his face.

"What are you doing?" Manny whispered.

"Ssh." I said.

He just shook his head.

I knew I had to be extra careful because everyone knew about Ms. Waverly's wandering eyes. She had what my dad calls googley-eyes. It's hard to tell which eye to focus on when she's talking to you because both eyes move independently of each other. It is a well known fact that Ms. Waverly can sit at her desk and grade papers with one eye while the other eye scans the classroom looking for students who are misbehaving.

I bent the end of each straw carefully, so it would fit into the next straw. So far, I had three finished. This was taking longer than I thought. Ten minutes had passed and I was finally done. I passed a note to Manny that said "Cough really loud at 10:10 exactly, pass it on." He nodded and I watched the note pass from hand to hand to hand. It was 10:07. I sat nervously at my desk and tried to look like I was working on math as my hand crept into the pocket of my jeans. My index finger curled around the pop-tab of the lemon-lime soda that rested in my pant's pocket.

Finally, the clock reached 10:10 and the whole class began coughing. I quickly popped the soda tab and shoved the straws in while the class coughed away. The sound of the popping lid was muffled by everyone coughing. Ms. Waverly knew something was up, but I could tell she wasn't sure what it was.

"Are we all coming down with colds today?" she asked knowingly.

Twenty guilty eyes stared back at her silently.

"Perhaps we should skip recess. I would hate to take sick students outside," she added.

"But sunshine is good for sick kids," Eddie piped up.

"Is that so? Well, I don't see a lot of sunshine today. Just lots of clouds, maybe some sunshine on the horizon," she said as she stood up and peered out the window.

This was a perfect opportunity, Ms. Waverly had her back to us. With the straws in the can, I greedily sucked down the lemon-lime soda.

"Best not to take the chance…" Ms. Waverly added.

Groans from around the class, except from me. I was sipping soda as quickly as I could.

Ms. Waverly spun around just as I pushed the straw out of my mouth. I could tell Manny wanted to laugh, but he was holding it together.

"However, if we work hard on our math without any more silly interruptions, we may be able to go outside," she finished and sat down at her desk.

She always knew just what to do to get the class back in line. It was probably a good thing that Eddie was in her class because he had a reputation for making teachers cry or yell. Ms. Waverly never did either. She was stone-cold. Eddie had met his match.

I shoved the straws in my desk and started working on my math sheet. I knew I'd guzzled enough lemon-lime soda to create a massive burp. I felt the pressure in my chest. I opened my mouth to let out the world's biggest burp, but all that came out was a small hiccup.

It's a well known fact that any bodily function, no matter how small, can instantly disrupt a classroom full of fifth graders. And my hiccups would not stop! I continued to hiccup every ten seconds or so. Everyone laughed after each one.

Finally, Ms. Waverly said, "Josh, go drink some water."

I had to be very careful when I left the classroom, because I still had half of a can of soda left in my pocket. I walked to the drinking fountain, but then had a better idea. I snuck into the boy's bathroom, and hid in a stall. I figured if I chugged the rest of the soda, I might turn my hiccups into a burp. I chugged the rest of the can and threw it away in the trash. Let the custodian figure that one out! My hiccups stopped, so I headed back to class.

I took my seat quickly and continued to work on my math. Once again I felt the pressure in my chest. This was it!

"Hiccuuup!" It was the highest hiccup I had ever heard! The class exploded into laughter as I continued my ear-splitting, incredibly girly-sounding hiccups.

"You hiccup like a girl," Eddie said and laughed.

Smack! Ms. Waverly slammed a ruler on her desk. She had a smirk on her lips, so I could tell she wasn't really mad, she just wanted the class to settle down.

"Josh, go see Nurse Turley," she said as the class quieted down.

I had never been so embarrassed in my life. There was only one other time I could recall being this embarrassed in front of my classmates. It was during our second grade field trip to the zoo. A group of us were watching the monkeys and Eddie was teasing them. It was weird but you could tell the monkeys didn't like him. He reached into his lunch bag and pulled out a banana. I knew what he was going to do. I pointed to the sign that read, "Please don't feed the animals!"

Eddie didn't care. He threw the banana at the biggest monkey and it landed right in front of him. You could tell the monkey was not happy. Before we could all high-tail it out of the monkey area, the big monkey picked up Eddie's banana and sent it sailing right back at him. Apparently monkeys don't have the best aim because instead of hitting Eddie, that banana whacked me on the back of my head so hard that I fell down and skinned both my knees and had to go to the zoo's first aid station. I guess I shouldn't have been running away. Anyway, everyone laughed especially Eddie. He even wrote his zoo report on how monkeys should be used as designated pitchers during the World Series.

I tried to block out this awful memory as I walked down the hallway to the Nurse's Office. My hiccups reverberated off the walls and sounded even louder. I think I even heard an echo. Since all the classrooms had their doors open, I heard laughter from every room I passed. And not from just the students, I think I heard some teachers laughing, too.

Nurse Turley stood in the doorway of the Nurse's Office.

"I heard you all the way down the hall," she said as she scooted me into the office and made me sit on the uncomfortable bed again.

She leaned in close and examined my face, "Did you try drinking some water?"

I nodded yes, trying not to breath. *Did she ever eat anything beside tuna fish?*

"Did you guzzle any food or drink? Anything before getting your hiccups?"

"No," I said innocently.

"Hum, I know one thing we can try…it might not work…but keep an open…**BOO**!"

"Aaah!" I screamed.

She watched me for what seemed like twenty minutes but it was probably closer to twenty seconds.

"That's the oldest trick in the book! A good scare works every time." she laughed.

"Hiccup," was my only reply.

"Oh darn. Try holding your breath. Take a deep breath and hold it for as long as you can." Nurse Turley said.

I took a deep breath and watched the second hand on the clock. When it got to eighteen seconds, I hiccupped. Nurse Turley frowned.

"Well, these things sometimes have to run their course. Although I did hear of a case where a man had hiccups for sixty-eight years."

Sixty-eight years? What had I gotten myself into?

I sat on the hard bed for fifteen minutes and I still hiccupped every minute or so. At least they were slowing down. Once again, my eyes were drawn to the rashes and chicken pox poster. It was truly disgusting. One photo showed a kid with severe poison ivy all over his arm. It made my skin itch and I scratched my arm in the same spot. Nurse Turley left for a moment and came back with Ms. Behr, our school counselor.

"Hi Josh," she said and pulled up a seat next to the hard bed. "I hear you have a nasty case of the hiccups."

"I guess so," I said and hiccupped.

"I was just wondering what you were doing before your hiccups began?" she asked.

"Math," I answered.

"Do you like math?"

"Yeah,"

"You don't have any trouble with math, do you?" she pried.

"No, I'm good at it."

"Oh," she said and looked perplexed. "Is there anything that has been bothering you lately?"

"Not really," I lied. I wasn't going to tell her about the bet and lose the room. "What does this have to do with hiccups?"

"Nurse Turley said you didn't eat or drink anything before your hiccups started, so I was thinking they may be stress hiccups."

"I never heard of that."

"Me neither, it's just a theory I have," she added.

Boy, was she weird.

"How's everything at home?"

"Okay," I decided to keep my answers short. Ms. Behr was notoriously long-winded. She could talk for days and it was almost lunch time. Bingo! I just had a thought. I knew a way to get out of this that was worthy of Eddie, the master liar.

"Ms. Behr, sometimes I get the hiccups at home, too. Mostly when I get stressed out. I guess having Eddie move in with me has been kind of stressful. But as soon as I eat something they go away."

"I know blended families can sometimes cause undue stress. Perhaps I should counsel you and Eddie together for a few days," she said.

"What?" I yelled. "I mean, that's okay. I'm fine really. I just need some lunch."

"I'll see you both tomorrow during recess. It will be our first session. Now, go to lunch."

"Hiccup," was all I could say.

CHAPTER 5

The next day, Eddie and I made our way down the hall to counseling. I could tell he was mad. "You feel like punching me, don't you?" I goaded him. I knew if he was mean to me, I would automatically win the bet.

Eddie was surprisingly quiet.

"Well," I said again, "don't you?"

Eddie stopped right in front of Ms. Behr's door and blocked my way in. "Listen good, Josh. I'm not happy about missing recess and I don't know what you're pulling by having us both go to counseling but whatever it is, I will find out. I'm clever, like a prairie dog."

"Don't you mean clever like a fox?" I said.

"What? Why a fox?" Eddie asked.

I can't believe I had to live with him. "A fox, that's how the saying goes. Clever like a fox."

"Never heard that saying, but I doubt that foxes are smarter than prairie dogs. I watched this show on the Discovery Channel about prairie dogs and they actually understand human language. That's why I said clever like a prairie dog. Funny, you're the one who gets straight A's and I am the one who always seems to know more things."

"Whatever," I said. Now I wanted to punch him.

*　　　*　　　*

Ms. Behr greeted us with a smile and scooted us inside. "I'm sorry you boys are missing your recess, but this was the only free time I had today," she explained.

"Ms. Behr, I thought that kids were supposed to get 30 minutes of exercise each day. Isn't it a state law or something?" Eddie asked.

"Yes, as a matter of fact it is," Ms. Behr said looking very perplexed.

"So, you should pull us out of math class, not out of recess," Eddie challenged.

"I don't think pulling you out of math class is a good idea," Ms. Behr answered.

"Yeah, plus we already had PE today for 30 minutes," I added.

I realize my error too late as Eddie shot me a "you're dead" look.

Ms. Behr's office was filled with bookshelves, plush toys and rocking chairs. According to her, the rocking motion helped "relax the soul". I guess she needed to "relax her soul" too, because she was rocking away. That made me more nervous. *Why did she have to relax?* Maybe she didn't know what she was doing. Maybe she was scared of Eddie, he always had a weird effect on teachers. Eddie, however, seemed as cool as a cucumber. For some reason, grown-ups never ruffled his feathers.

Ms. Behr stopped rocking for a moment and put her elbows on her knees. "So, boys how's it going?"

"Everything's great," Eddie said.

"Not too bad," I mumbled. I felt very uncomfortable. And what was that smell? I noticed the plug-in air freshener and knew at once. Those flowering-smelly things always made my eyes tear up and my nose sniffle. I'm allergic to them and the smell was extra strong in this small office.

"Josh, yesterday when we talked, you said it was kind of stressful having Eddie move in with you. What did you mean?" she pried.

"Well, what I meant to say was that it was stressful, but it's okay now." I said.

She sat back and began rocking again. Her eyes peered into mine. "How was it stressful before?"

My eyes were tearing up from the air-freshener.

Ms. Behr put her hand on my shoulder. "It's okay Josh, just go with your feelings."

"Oh, okay. It was stressful, you know, unpacking boxes and all." I really sucked at lying. But the tears helped. Maybe I should try and breathe in more of the air freshener. I breathed in a gigantic gulp of air and started coughing.

Out of the corner of my eye, I saw Eddie trying not to smile. I wanted to signal him to jump in and help me but I knew Ms. Behr was watching us both like a hawk zeroing in on a mouse. Any type of signal or sign between us and she would know we were hiding something.

"Yeah, it's been kind of rough," Eddie said, finally.

Ms. Behr turned her attention to Eddie. I watched in amazement. Was he going to blow it?

"Go on," she said.

"See, it was just me and my mom for so long, I got used to having her to myself and now Josh comes along and I gotta share her." Eddie said.

"And how does that make you feel?" Ms. Behr asked.

Eddie put on his best sad face. "Sometimes it hurts me right here." Eddie pointed to his heart.

Ms. Behr turned to me. Eddie shrugged and smirked at me when Ms. Behr wasn't looking. He was faking! Brilliant!

"Oh yeah, well, I have to share my dad!" I said and started sniffing again. And this time is wasn't from the air freshener. I really did feel this way a little, I couldn't fake it like Eddie. But having Allie as a mom made up for it, though. And I knew Eddie liked spending time with my dad, too.

"And I have to share a room with him. And everything has to be perfect and in its place. He is some kind of neaty, freaky, nerd king," Eddie said.

Through my watery eyes and sniffles I answered, "Eddie's so sloppy. He leaves his stuff everywhere in our bedroom. I have to step over his stuff just to go to the bathroom. He's a giant pig!"

"Now Josh, we are not going to revert to name calling," Ms. Behr scolded.

Didn't Eddie just call me neaty, freaky, nerd king?
"Sorry," I mumbled.

"And Eddie, you can obviously tell that Josh is really upset," she said as she handed me a tissue.

Eddie studied me for a moment with a thoughtful expression on his face.

"Sorry, dude. I guess I wish that I was more organized like you. My mom's always on my case about it," he said and really seemed to mean it.

"It's okay, I should probably loosen up. That's what my dad says anyway," I answered.

The bell rang. Recess was over.

"You boys better get back to class. I'll see you tomorrow at recess time," Ms. Behr said.

Eddie looked horrified. Ms. Behr laughed, "Come on Eddie, you guys made some good progress today but we just scratched the surface. I know it's hard to give up your recess, but this is important."

Poor, Eddie. He loved recess. It was his time to shine. He was good at every game and was always picked first. Guess who was picked last.

Then suddenly I remembered what Eddie said earlier, "Ms. Behr tomorrow is art day."

"So?" she answered.

"We don't have PE tomorrow, we have art. So according to the state law, we need our 30 minutes of exercise time. That's recess tomorrow," I said very proud of myself for remembering.

"Of course, make it Friday then," she said and scooted us out the door.

"Good save, neaty, freaky, nerd-king," Eddie said and smiled. I didn't even mind the name-calling this time.

*   *   *

Eddie shoved a big forkful of tuna noodle casserole into his mouth. A little bit of the sauce clung to his chin. I didn't have much of an appetite. Probably because I spent the last two days in Nurse Turley's office smelling her tuna breath. I noticed she had an extra scoop of casserole on her tray when she walked by. Mystery solved.

"Hey Manny, you gonna eat that casserole?" Eddie said between bites.

"Naw, you can have it," Manny said and scooped it onto Eddie's tray.

"Thanks," Eddie said.

Eddie and I decided that we should start eating lunch together. Actually Eddie decided. He said it would break his mom's heart if she found out we didn't really eat together.

"How would she find out?" I asked him last night as we lay in our bunk beds.

"Oh, I'd tell her," he said.

"Eddie, that doesn't make any sense."

"Maybe not to you, but I told my mom we eat lunch together and I can't lie to her. So now we have to really eat lunch together."

"But you lied to her about why I ate those lemons and limes."

"It doesn't count if I lie for someone else, only if I lie for myself," he answered.

"I don't see the difference."

"Gosh, Josh, sometimes you can be so dumb," was all he said. I still didn't get it.

So, here we were, eating lunch together. At first I thought my friends would freak, but they didn't. They just stared when he sat down. It was kind of like when you see a stray dog. It's exciting because it could end up being your best friend or it could end up biting you. My friends were waiting to find out which kind of stray dog Eddie would be.

"I love tuna fish. If I lived in the ocean, that's all I would eat," Eddie said.

"If I lived in the ocean, I would be a shark," Paul added.

"Not me. I'd be a dolphin," Chelsea said.

"Me too, they're the smartest animals in the ocean," said Marina.

We sure are the center of interest today.

"No, they're not," Eddie replied.

"Really?" Marina asked surprised at not knowing something Eddie knew.

"Well, maybe they are but if I had to be an animal in the ocean I'd be an octopus," he answered.

Everyone laughed but not Eddie. He didn't even get mad. *What was going on?* The old Eddie would have flattened anyone who so much as mocked him.

"Yeah, they're kind of funny looking, but they're the hunters of the sea. They can build a shelter from stuff just floating around the ocean and hide under it until a fish comes along. Then BAM! They gobble it up. And they can change their body color in seconds. They can even change the pattern of their skin. It's like they have built in camouflage. It's true. I saw it on Animal Planet," Eddie said.

"Wow," Manny said impressed by Eddie's knowledge.

"That's cool," Paul added.

"I'd still be a dolphin," Marina said.

Seriously, what was going on? My friends were listening to Eddie. I guess I should have been happy. At least he didn't bite them.

Eddie the Octopus

CHAPTER 6

"**Y**ou don't have to drink soda to burp really loud," the guy on the internet video said. *You don't? I've been doing it the hard way.*

"First, you have to swallow lots of air," he said and started gulping air. I remembered seeing Eddie do this before each burp. That had to be it!

Gulp. Gulp. I gulped air. It felt kind of weird like something was stuck in my throat.

"Buuuuuuuuurp!" The guy on the video let out a huge burp. It had to be at least twenty seconds long. Actually, it was kind of gross.

Gulp. Gulp. I kept gulping air.

"After a while, you will get good enough to talk through your burps," the internet burping whiz said. "Let me demonstrate."

He gulped lots of air and then burped the ABC's. Wow, he got all the way to the letter J!

I kept gulping.

"You can also impress your friends with full sentences," he said and gulped more air. "Hello, how are you?" he said through a long burp. This guy was awesome.

Finally, I felt something funny in my throat. It felt like all the air was coming back up. "Buurp!" I did it! It wasn't super long, but I finally did it. Now I just had to practice, so I could burp really loud and long. I'd win the bet yet.

"Hey shrimp," Eddie said as he entered our room. "I've seen that video. That guy is okay, I guess." He shrugged.

"Oh, he's more than okay, he's a burping professional," I said. "He can burp the ABC's."

"You mean like this?" Eddie gulped a few times and then burped; "A-B-C-D-E-F-G-H-I-J-K-L-M-N-O-P."

Eddie really was the master. The internet guy only got to J, Eddie got to P. I gulped some air and tried, "A-B-C…"

"Not bad, for a girl," Eddie teased.

"Shut up, Eddie. I know your secret. And now I can master it, too," I said.

"But can you master it by Friday? That's two days away. Maybe, but maybe not."

"I think you should be more worried about being nice to everyone in the school before Friday."

"I don't have to be nice to everyone, just the people I've been mean to in the past," Eddie said. "I'm doing pretty good."

"Really?"

"Yeah, I haven't taken any money or scared anyone all week."

"That's not the same as being nice, that's just being normal. You haven't really done anything nice for anyone other than leave them alone."

42

Eddie looked confused and a little nervous. "So you're saying I have to do something nice for the people I've been mean to?"

"That's right."

"But how will I know who they are? What if I was mean to somebody once and then I forgot about it. Would I lose the bet if I didn't do something nice for that person?"

"Yep."

"But that could be the whole school!"

"Including teachers," I added.

"Including teachers?" Eddie said, looking defeated.

"And the custodians, the principal, and secretary," I said smugly. For the first time, I thought I might actually win the bet.

"Crud," he said.

"Oh, and the lunch ladies, too," I said to rub it in.

"I'm always nice to them. I'm their best customer. They love me." Eddie smiled slyly.

"What?" I asked.

"Nothing, nothing at all," he answered, still smiling mischievously.

I didn't like the look of that smile. He'd just figured something out. Why did I feel like I'd just blown it again?

*   *   *

Gulp. Gulp. I gulped air as I rode the bus. It was Thursday morning and I was going win the bet today. I was going to let loose the biggest burp Ms. Waverly and my class had ever heard.

The bus pulled up to the school and stopped. The brakes hissed loudly. A couple of girls were jumping rope. Eddie stopped to listen to their jump rope rhyme. I'd heard it before but I didn't think Eddie had. If anything was going to make him mad, it was that particular song. Usually when girls sang this song, they would stop when they saw Eddie. This time they didn't. Maybe because he wasn't bullying anyone this week and they weren't afraid. I stood next to Eddie because I wanted to see what would happen.

> *Mean ole Eddie, loves his spaghetti.*
> *Goes to sleep and wets his bed-die.*
> *That's not funny, weighs a ton-nie*
> *How many times can he take our money?*
> *1...2...3...4...5...*

Eddie nudged me in the ribs with his elbow. "Hey, that's pretty funny, and true. Except the part about wetting the bed. That's not funny at all. Not even a little."

"Aren't you going to do something about it?" I asked.

"No, not this week. Plus, they're little girls. What are they first graders? Second graders? Come on, Josh. How big of a bully do you think I am?"

"Do you really want me to answer that?"

"Probably not," he said.

*   *   *

Gulp. Gulp. I walked down the hallway. I could feel the pressure building in my gut. Eddie looked worried as he entered the classroom.

44

I diverted down the hallway to the restroom. I kept gulping air and checked my watch.

"7:58," I murmured between gulps. "Two more minutes." I knew I had to wait until 8:00 so everyone was in the classroom. I didn't want to lose the bet because someone hadn't arrived at school yet. I had to burp in front of the whole class for it to count.

It was 7:59, close enough. I walked into the classroom. I could barely hold the burp back. It felt like an air volcano was about to erupt out of my mouth. I walked through the door...

"Buuuuuuuuuuuurp!" Wow, that was the best one I ever did! The class burst into laughter. A few students even applauded. I looked at Eddie. He was laughing, too. Why was he laughing? He just lost the bet.

I turned to look at Ms. Waverly. I figured she'll probably scold me and that was all.

"Oh, no," I said aloud.

"Oh, no, is right young man," a tall witch-like creature cackled.

It was Ms. Sniedendorf, the meanest substitute teacher ever!

"Sniedendorf," I whispered before I realized I said it out loud.

"You will be spending the day with me," she said.

Torturous. Ms. Sniedendorf was a legend. Everyone knew her plan. Each time she subbed, she picked a boy or girl who was goofing off and used them as an example. They had to spend the entire day with her. Even lunch! Usually it was Eddie, but not today.

She pointed to a small student desk right next to Ms. Waverly's desk. I walked over and caught Eddie's eye. He was smirking.

"Doesn't count," he mouthed and I knew he was right. The rules were that I had to burp in front of the class and Ms. Waverly. Kind of hard to do because Ms. Waverly was absent.

"Perhaps I should mention your behavior to Mr. Duff," she added. "Such a rude young man. When I was a full-time teacher, a child would have been paddled for such behavior."

She was so old. I couldn't believe she used to paddle kids. I think that may be considered child abuse.

*   *   *

The rest of the day was uneventful except for art class. We were drawing a still-life. Mr. Cutler, our art teacher, had set up an arrangement of sports equipment on a table in the middle of the room. We had to draw it as best as we could. I concentrated on my drawing. It wasn't going well. My basketball looked more like a football. Art wasn't my best subject. I glanced over at Eddie's still-life. It was really good.

"Nice use of space and proportion, Eddie," Mr. Cutler said as he made his rounds. Eddie beamed. Art was Eddie's second best subject. PE was his first.

"Josh, try to draw the basketball as a circle instead of an oval." I erased and tried again. "Much better," he said and moved on. Even though it wasn't a compliment like Eddie got, at least Mr. Cutler wasn't making my life miserable like Ms. Sniedendorf was.

When Mr. Cutler was out of earshot Eddie asked, "Hey Josh. How was lunch?"

"Ha-ha very funny," I answered. I had to spend lunch with Ms. Sniedendorf. That really killed my appetite.

"I know, it's awful," Eddie snickered.

He would know too, considering it was usually him who had to sit with Sniedendorf.

"Did you notice how she wipes her mouth after every bite?" he whispered.

"Yeah, what's with that?"

"I guess she's a lady," Eddie said in a girly voice.

I laughed. "And do you know what else? She was eating this sandwich with this weird looking meat on it. I overheard Coach Fox ask her what kind of lunchmeat it was and Sniedendorf said it was head cheese."

"What's that?" Eddie whispered.

"Sniedendorf said it was made from the brains of a pig."

"Nasty, even I wouldn't eat that," Eddie said and laughed too loud.

Mr. Cutler gave us the raised eyebrow. That's the universal teacher sign for "you're skating on thin ice". We finished our still-life drawings quietly. Mr. Cutler put Eddie's still-life on the board as a good example. It really was the best one.

CHAPTER 7

"Cinnamon rolls," Eddie said from the top bunk on Friday morning.

We both jumped out of bed and hurried to get ready. Eddie and I don't have much in common, but we both love cinnamon rolls.

"Out of my way." Eddie pushed by me because I beat him to the top of the stairs. He knew the first one to the kitchen would get the best roll. The one with the most icing.

"No fair," I said.

Eddie's big feet clomped down the stairs. He spread his arms out so I couldn't get by. My dad watched from the kitchen.

"In a bit of a hurry today, Eddie?" my dad asked.

"Yeah, I love cinnamon rolls," he answered.

"I noticed from your behavior on the stairs," my dad added.

"Sorry, I guess I got carried away. Josh can pick first," Eddie said.

My dad ruffled Eddie's hair. "Good sport," he said and Eddie smiled.

Good sport? My dad gave me one of those looks that meant let it go. I grabbed the gooiest cinnamon roll and a glass of cold milk and sat down to eat.

I noticed that Eddie always listened to my dad. He didn't talk back to him either. It was weird. Most kids would be mad if some guy married their mom and tried to take their dad's place. Eddie didn't seem to mind. Maybe it was because my dad was so much nicer than Eddie's dad. I met Eddie's dad once and he was kind of a jerk. He kept punching me in the arm and calling me little-man. He said boys should be tough, but the arm punching kind of hurt. My dad told him to lay off.

We finished our cinnamon rolls and headed for the bus stop.

"Today's the last day," I said.

"Yep," Eddie said.

"All I have to do is burp in front of the class."

"You're going to get so busted after what you did yesterday," Eddie laughed.

"I have a plan for that."

I decided to wait until 2:59 to burp really loud. That way when the dismissal bell rang at 3:00, Ms. Waverly would only have one minute to react. I was hoping that since it was Friday, she'd let it go. It was risky to wait, but it might work. The only way my plan wouldn't work was if Ms. Waverly was absent again today.

"What's your plan, shrimpo?" Eddie asked.

"Wouldn't you like to know?" I answered.

"Duh, I just asked you, so of course I want to know. Sometimes you're kind of stupid."

"What about you? How are you going to be nice to the entire school in one day?"

"Wouldn't you like to know? Oh, now I get it!" he laughed. "You were joking before."

"Come on, genius." I laughed as we boarded the bus.

*   *   *

Bony knuckles grabbed my shoulder as I walked into the classroom. It was Ms. Waverly.

"I heard you had a rough day yesterday according to the note that Ms. Sniedendorf left," she said.

"Yes, Ma'am," I replied.

"Hopefully, you'll have a better day today." Ms. Waverly frowned.

I scooted into the classroom and sat down. This was going to be a long day. Maybe Eddie would blow his dare. Eddie hadn't come to class yet. If he was late, he would get a tardy slip. We got off the bus at the same time. *Why wasn't he in class?*

RINGGGG! RINGGGG!

Oh my gosh! That was the bell. Eddie was going to get in so much trouble. I hoped he wouldn't get grounded again. Wait! *Why did I care?* I wasn't his friend, although it had been kind of fun hanging out with him lately. *What was happening to me?* I wanted Eddie to get into trouble. I wanted that attic room!

After Ms. Waverly took attendance, Eddie strolled into the classroom. I could see a note in his hand. What was he up to?

"I'm sorry I'm late, but I have a note from the lunch ladies explaining my tardiness." Eddie handed the note to Ms. Waverly.

Ms. Waverly read the note. "Well, I will certainly look forward to lunch today. Thank you, Eddie. You may take your seat."

Eddie grinned. He looked at me and gave me the thumbs up sign. I felt like puking.

*　　　　*　　　　*

"Wow, free ice cream everybody!" A first grader shouted as he left the cafetorium at lunch time.

"We get free ice cream?" Manny asked as we stood in line for lunch.

"I hope so," I said thinking I could sure use a break today. I stopped the first grader. "Hey kid, did you say we get free ice cream?"

"Yeah," he answered and wiped off the chocolate ice cream mustache above his lip. "It's great. That big, mean guy is buying everyone ice cream today."

"What big, mean guy?" I asked but I already knew the answer.

"You know, that guy Eddie," the first grader grinned.

"Oh, no," I sighed as I grabbed my lunch tray. At the checkout Ms. Betty, the lunch lady, told me to choose chocolate, vanilla or strawberry delight, compliments of Eddie. I didn't want to help Eddie, but I took some strawberry anyway. Hey, it's free ice cream. I entered the lunchroom.

Eddie was smiling from ear to ear. He waved me over to what now had become our usual table.

Everywhere I looked, kids were eating ice cream. Even the principal and teachers were eating ice cream. I felt cold all over. It must have been all the ice cream, or maybe I got a chill when I realized Eddie just won the bet. Unless I can burp today…

"How's your ice cream?" Eddie asked everybody at the table.

"It's delicious," Marina replied between spoonfuls of vanilla.

"Yeah, thanks Eddie, that sure was nice of you," Paul added.

"Did you hear that, Josh? Paul said it was nice of me." Eddie smirked.

Just then, Mr. Duff, the principal walked over to us. "Edward, that was a very generous thing you did today buying the whole school ice cream." He smiled at Eddie and walked away while eating his cup of strawberry delight.

Strawberry Delight Ice Cream

"I can't believe you bought the whole school ice cream," Chelsea said. "That must have cost a lot of money."

"Just about everything in my piggy bank," Eddie said and grinned.

"Wow, you must have had a lot of money saved up," Manny said.

"Yeah, I'm a saver," Eddie answered.

"Of other people's money," I added under my breath.

Everyone gasped and looked at Eddie to see how he would respond. The old Eddie would have flattened me but this new Eddie just looked at me with a hurt expression.

"I guess Josh doesn't know who my favorite medieval hero is. I was watching a movie last night about him and thought to myself, how can I be more like him? What could I do that would be like something he would do? And, presto! It came to me; buy the whole school ice cream."

"What hero?" Marina asked.

"What movie?" Paul added.

Before Eddie could answer, I jumped in. "Hey, you didn't watch a movie last night. You had to stay up late and do homework, remember?" Hah! I got him.

"Josh, it just so happens that in-between my homework breaks, I was "sneak" watching a movie in the bathroom so I wouldn't get busted. Thank you very much."

Dang. I wondered why the portable DVD player was set up in the bathroom.

"Was it a movie about Santa Claus?" Manny asked.

"No. Though I do admire his love of milk and cookies." Eddie laughed. The whole table laughed with him.

"Then who?" Marina inquired.

"Robin Hood, of course. He takes from the rich and gives to the needy. And I thought, who isn't needy for ice cream?!" They all cheered.

Eddie was on fire.

*　　　*　　　*

I rubbed my eyes to keep the air freshener in Ms. Behr's office from making them water. It helped a little. Away we rocked on our rocking chairs.

"Well, boys, how's it going at home?" she pried.

"Okay," I mumbled.

"Pretty good," Eddie said.

"What's good about it Eddie?" she asked.

"We get a lot more cable channels at this house," Eddie answered.

"Is that all?" she asked.

"No. Jack plays ball with me when he gets home."

"I see. And does he play ball with you, Josh?" she asked.

"Sometimes," I answered.

"Why only sometimes?"

"I like to get my homework done," I replied.

"When do you do your homework, Eddie?" she inquired.

"In between commercials," I answered and laughed. Eddie glared.

"Is that true?" Ms. Behr's brow wrinkled in concern.

54

"Pretty much. See, I need to take breaks during my homework, say every ten minutes or so. Then I concentrate really hard on my homework for about five minutes during commercials. It takes a little longer but it's how I roll," he said and shrugged. Ms. Behr looked confused.

"I see," she said not convinced, although I have witnessed Eddie doing this myself. I had to admit, ever since Eddie started doing his own homework, this method did seem to work for him.

"By the way, Eddie, thanks for the ice cream today," she gushed.

"You're very welcome, Ms. Behr," he replied.

"What made you decide to do that?"

Eddie started in on his long spiel about Robin Hood. Wow. He could snow anyone! Ms. Behr was enthralled by Eddie's change of heart story. I dabbed at my irritated eyes.

"So Josh," she turned her focused gaze on me. "Tell me about the problem with Ms. Sniedendorf yesterday."

"It wasn't really a problem, I just had a little indigestion," I answered.

Ms. Behr pulled out the note written by Ms. Sniedendorf that she'd left for Ms. Waverly yesterday. She scanned it while talking out loud, "No major problems…completed math assignment…assigned additional math…Ah, here it is; Josh Miller was very rude. He purposely burped in front of the whole class to test my authority. I recommend swift action and parental involvement."

"I didn't try to test her authority or whatever she said! I just burped. It just came out," I said.

Ms. Behr turned to Eddie. "Eddie will you excuse us, I'd like to talk to Josh alone. You can go to recess."

"Woo-ho!" Eddie yelled and leapt out of the chair. He left Ms. Behr's office. From behind her back, he made an L shape with his finger and thumb on his forehead and mouthed the word "Loser" to me. Jerk.

"Now Josh, Ms. Sniedendorf would sometimes sub for my teacher when I was a little girl and I know how tough she can be," Ms. Behr said.

Wow, Sniededorf subbed when Ms. Behr was a little girl? She really was old! Ms. Behr was no spring chicken. Maybe Sniedendorf was a witch for real.

"I also know she wouldn't misinterpret what happened. So why did you burp on purpose yesterday?" she asked.

"I don't know," I answered trying to stall for time. I couldn't let her find out about the bet.

"Eddie's getting quite popular lately," she added.

So what? Why is she bringing up Eddie?

"I know he is a little rough around the edges. Are you trying to be more like him by burping?"

Perfect, I'm in! "Yeah, you got me Ms. Behr. I'm trying to be more like Eddie," I said.

"I'm glad you are looking up to Eddie, but you must remain true to yourself. Now don't cry everything will be just fine." She patted my knee and handed me a tissue.

I wiped my eyes and looked at the air freshener. This was kind of working in my favor. I decided to go with it. "I'll try to be true to myself, Ms. Behr. It's kind of hard sometimes. Eddie's so cool," I said through my tears.

"You just keep on keeping on, Josh. Now go to class."

What does that mean? Grown-ups are weird.

"Okay, I'll try. But I can't promise it will be easy. I may have the urge to be like Eddie and forget to control it," I said setting myself up for the big burp this afternoon. Now Ms. Behr will have my back and can explain my gross behavior to Ms. Waverly. I felt as crafty as Eddie. Oh, no! Maybe I did want to be like Eddie! No, I just wanted the new room I told myself as I walked back to class.

*   *   *

"Thanks again." Manny patted Eddie's shoulder on the way to his desk.

"No problem." Eddie said.

"Yeah, the ice cream was awesome!" Matthew grinned at Eddie.

Eddie saluted him. I mean he actually saluted. This afternoon was becoming unbearable.

"Okay class, our last report today will be from Marina." Ms. Waverly snapped the class back to order.

Marina rushed up to the front of the class. "For my biography report I chose Ronald Reagan," Marina said and started reading.

I really did try to pay attention, but it was kind of boring. I guess he was once president or an actor or something. Usually I like Marina's reports, but today I was more concerned about watching the clock. I had to plan my burp at exactly the right time. The seconds on the clock ticked by slowly. So very slowly.

"And then he got shot in the head," Marina said.

What, who got shot in the head? Ronald Reagan?
Dang, Marina's report was getting good but I missed it
because of the stupid clock.

Marina continued, "But he survived."

Oh, maybe I didn't miss that much. I turned my
gaze to the window. The wind had picked up and the
sky was getting more and more gray, just like my
mood. I spotted a spider's web on the window sill and
watched it waving back and forth in the wind. How did
it stand the wind gusts? They were so strong. The wind
blew the web up and down like the parachute in PE
class. It was cool. The little spider was tucked into the
thickest part of the web. Insects are so smart.

Because I was so engrossed in watching the
spider's web I didn't realize Marina had finished her
report until I heard everyone clapping.

"Thank you, Marina," Ms. Waverly said.

Marina took a little bow. Sometimes she was
such a showoff. I looked at the clock. Oh no! It was
2:45. I quickly started gulping air to get ready for my big
burp.

Ms. Waverly said, "Students, please grab your
backpacks and pack-up for the day." Everyone leapt
out of their chairs. I packed-up but kept gulping air.

After everyone was packed and back in their
seats, I took my final gulp. I could feel a big burp
brewing. It was 2:56. I looked over at Eddie and
noticed he was gulping air too.

What was going on? Why was he gulping?

I almost lost my nerve. I started gulping again. I
gulped faster and faster. It was 2:58, close enough. I
opened my mouth and let out the world's biggest
burp. At the same time Eddie opened his mouth and
burped, too. We were having a dueling burping

contest. That was his plan all along. He was going to distract half of the class with his burp so I'd lose.

I knew I had to burp longer than Eddie. *Could I do it?* I could feel my burp starting to wane.

I swear Eddie was enjoying this. He was swaying back and forth while he was burping and his eyes looked as if they were smiling.

I pushed every little bit of the burp out of my throat. The entire class sat with their mouths open. The students near me were watching me but the students near Eddie were watching him. I had to get them all to watch me.

Finally, a miracle happened. Eddie stopped burping and I kept going. I had out-burped the master! All eyes were on me. I had done it!

Ms. Waverly looked shocked and then she turned her back on the whole class. I saw her shoulders begin to shake. *Was she laughing?*

The bell rang and I sprinted out of class.

*　　　*　　　*

The rain pelted down on us as we ran to the buses. I didn't mind at all. I felt invincible. Instead of making a fuss over Eddie, everyone was surrounding me.

"Nice job." Manny high-fived me.

"Yeah, way cool. I can't believe you did that." Paul shouted as he headed for the bus. I gave him one of Eddie's salutes. It felt great.

"That was disgusting," Marina said, temporarily interrupting my good mood. "Why'd you have to do that right after my report? Do you know how long I worked on it? Well, do you?"

I didn't know if she actually wanted an answer or not, so I just shrugged my shoulders. She just shook her head and jumped on the bus.

Eddie blocked my way up the bus stairs. "Well shrimp, it looks like we both completed our dares this week."

"Yeah," I said wiping the rain out of my face. "No thanks to you. Why'd you have to burp at the same time?"

Eddie moved over so I could get on the bus. He followed me to my seat.

"It's all for the love of competition," Eddie said.

I said, "I hate competition."

"I know. I can't believe you out-burped me."

"I know. I can't believe it either. It was fair right? You didn't stop on purpose did you?" I asked him.

"Why would I do that? I would have won the room this week, fair and square. Do you really think I want to do dares for the next two weeks?" Eddie asked me.

I noticed a smile creep around the edges of his mouth. I didn't answer him because I was afraid that yes, he really did want to do dares for the next two weeks.

CHAPTER 8

I woke up earlier than Eddie. I had a restless night of sleep. Something was gnawing at me about Eddie's bet and I couldn't put a finger on it. He didn't bully anyone at school and he did buy everyone ice cream. So what was it? I got it!

"Eddie, Eddie. Wake up." I climbed up the ladder and tried shaking his shoulders. He didn't even stop snoring. I tried again, this time really putting some muscle behind it.

He stirred a little. "What? I'm trying to sleep, it's Saturday." He wiped some drool from the side of his mouth with the back of his pajama sleeve. He must have been dreaming about cupcakes. I've seen him practically drool over them before.

"Hey, you didn't win the bet. The room is mine," I said.

That did it. He bolted upright so fast he almost hit his head on the ceiling. "What are you talking about, I won my dare without cheating."

"Well, not really," I said.

Eddie thought for a moment and said, "Who was I mean to?" He looked concerned, yet he really didn't know. "Who?" he asked again.

I felt a little embarrassed but I said, "Me. You were mean to me all week."

"No I wasn't. What are you talking about?"

Apparently, Eddie didn't remember. "Well, you called me dumb, shrimp, stupid and you made the "loser" sign at me. You…"

"Hold on, hold on," Eddie interrupted. "That wasn't being mean, that's called teasing. Don't you know the difference?"

"No." It didn't feel like there was a difference.

"Josh, there's a huge difference. Teasing is what brothers do," he said.

"But we're not brothers."

Eddie's face fell. He actually looked hurt and I could tell he wasn't faking.

"I mean we're not real brothers, we're step-brothers," I said.

"I don't see the difference between the two," he said honestly.

"Well, then you're dumber than I thought," I said cautiously, trying out this teasing thing.

Eddie's face froze and then broke into a huge smile. "Oh, now you're teasing me, good job." He patted my shoulder.

I laughed with him. Maybe brothers do tease each other.

*   *   *

Up in the attic, the air smelled like sawdust.

"Starting to look good, don't you think?" my dad asked.

"Yeah, I like the wood ceiling. It's cool. Like we're in a log cabin," I answered.

"The room should be finished in a couple of weeks. Have you two decided who gets to move in yet?" my dad asked.

"We're working on it," Eddie answered. My dad looked a little skeptical but just nodded.

Eddie was supposed to have spent the weekend with his dad and his dad's new girlfriend, but at the last minute his dad cancelled with some lame excuse. My Eddie-free weekend was no more. Eddie didn't seem to mind, however.

"This place is huge. You could fit a big bed and a dresser in here and still have room for a video game area and computer. And look there." Eddie pointed to a blank wall. "That wall would be perfect for my gigantic eagle poster."

"It would," I said, although I didn't mean to say it out loud.

"What?" Eddie asked. "You agree with me?"

"No, no. I mean it would be good for my poster," I quickly said.

"You don't have any posters."

"Um, yeah, I do. You just haven't seen them. They're awesome." Note to self, get some cool posters and fast.

"Okay, boys, that's enough. Yes, this attic is big. Big enough for two boys to share," my dad added.

"No way," Eddie and I said at the same time.

"Alright, it was just a suggestion," my dad said and looked somewhat disappointed.

I know my dad wanted Eddie and me to get along, but it wasn't going to happen. Sure, we had been spending more time together, but that was just because of the bet. Or was it because we were becoming brothers, like Eddie said? Anyway, it would soon be over and I would have my new room all to myself. My thoughts were interrupted by a disgusting smell.

"Gross, Eddie," I gasped.

"What? Can I help it if I had some bean dip for a snack last night?" he asked innocently.

Even my dad made a face. "I'll think I'll go downstairs," he said and quickly left.

"You better start eating beans if you want to win next week's bet," Eddie said and laughed.

"You're giving me pointers?"

"I dunno, am I?" he smirked.

What was that supposed to mean?

"Smell you later, Josh," Eddie said and stomped down the stairs with his giant feet.

"Yes, you will smell me later. Later this week," I said.

*   *   *

"My Josh, you are up early. Is everything alright?" Allie asked on Monday morning.

I sat down at the breakfast table. "Um, yeah. I was hoping to get a really big, nutritious breakfast this morning."

"You mean you don't want your usual cereal and toast?"

"Right. I think I need ham and eggs. A huge plate. I'm having a growth spurt and I need extra protein for my body." I took a sip of orange juice.

64

I could see Allie size me up. I'm sure I didn't look any taller and she didn't say anything but, "Okay, ham and eggs it is." And then she went to the fridge to get breakfast.

The smell of ham and eggs made my stomach rumble. As soon as Allie set down my plate, I immediately started eating. The ham was salty but delicious and the yellow egg yolk was rich and filling.

"Alright, my kinda breakfast," Eddie said as he sat down next to me with an even bigger plate than mine. "I guess you're fueling up for your big day," he laughed. "Good luck."

Something about the way he said good luck made me nervous. *Did Eddie know something that I didn't?*

"Maybe you should be more concerned about our poetry unit this week," I challenged.

Bull's eye! Now Eddie looked nervous. I mean really nervous.

Eddie put up a false front and said, "Well, yeah, I'll do fine." Then he added, "I'm the King of Rhyme."

"Okay, I get it," I said.

"Get what?"

"Fine and rhyme," I said and he still looked puzzled.

"What about them?"

"Duh, they rhyme. Well, kind of."

"Oh, yeah, they do. And I wasn't even trying! Cool." Eddie laughed.

I hated Mondays.

*   *   *

Ms. Waverly stood by the white board as she read the couplet she'd written.

If you are smart and work real hard
You'll write a couplet just like a bard.

"What's a bard?" Manny asked.

Eddie's hand flew into the air.

"Yes, Eddie?" Ms. Waverly looked doubtful.

"A bard is a poet from medieval times," he answered.

"Very good! You are the first student in thirty years that knew what a bard was. How did you know?"

"I went to this really cool festival with my mom once. It was called a Renaissance Faire and everyone dressed up like knights and princesses and stuff. And we saw this cool play called, 'Theatre in the Mud'. The actors had to perform in mud! It was awesome. They kept slipping and sliding and throwing mud at each other. They were really dirty when they were done."

"And what about the bard?"

Eddie continued, "Oh yeah. The bard strolled around the faire reciting poetry."

"Was he in the mud?"

"Ah, no. Why would the bard be in the mud?" Eddie asked Ms. Waverly.

"Never mind," Ms. Waverly said very frustrated. Eddie was good at confusing teachers.

Ms. Waverly placed us in groups of four to work on our couplets. She said since it was our first time writing, we could help each other. Eddie, Manny and Marina were in my group. I could tell Marina wasn't happy about being stuck in our group all week. I saw her glance at the group that Chelsea was in.

As soon as we took our spots, I felt the first rumblings in my stomach. Wow, those ham and eggs worked fast. I braced myself for a world class gas-fest. Unfortunately, all that came out was *POOF*. No one heard it. But, boy could they smell it!

"Oh my gosh, who SBD'd?" Marina cried.

"What's SBD?" Manny asked just as the smell assaulted his nostrils. "Oh, I get it. Silent but deadly, gross!"

My face turned the color of the fake glass apple that Ms. Waverly kept on her desk.

"It was me, you got a problem with it?" Eddie asked.

"No," Manny said.

Despite Eddie being nice lately, he could still intimidate our classmates. *But why was Eddie claiming my smell?*

"Let's just work on our couplets," Marina said, trying to cover her nose.

We all went back to work. I tried to think of something clever and funny but I couldn't concentrate because I was still wondering why Eddie claimed my awful, nasty fart. There had to be a reason. Eddie acted dumb, but he was a mastermind when it came to winning. After a few minutes had passed we decided to share our couplets. Manny went first.

> *I may be the shortest boy in the class,*
> *But when it comes to a race, I'm first and never last.*

"That's good," I said and it was true. Manny was the shortest boy in the class and he was the fastest. Even the teachers couldn't run as fast as Manny and he was the only boy I was taller than.

"The meter is off," Marina said.

"What?" Manny asked.

"The meter is wrong. If you count the beats or syllables, the first line has ten and the second line has thirteen. It doesn't flow well," she added.

Even though Marina was the smartest kid in our class she sometimes acted like a snob.

Manny looked crushed and Marina saw that she'd been too hard on him. "It's not bad, Manny. It's certainly true, too. Let me help you." She took his paper and made a few changes.

"Now listen to it," she said.

I may be the shortest boy in the class
But when I race, I'm the first not the last.

"Hey, that's much better," Manny brightened.

"Except that class and last don't truly rhyme," Marina added.

"Who cares, I like it. It's done," Manny said. "Let's hear yours, Marina."

Marina cleared her throat.

To write a couplet is my endeavor
It must be charming, witty and clever.

"That's good and it really rhymes," I said. "But what is an endeavor?"

"It's the name of one of the first space shuttles," Eddie offered. "It was actually named after a sea vessel, which is funny because the shuttle was going into space not into the ocean. Weird, huh? Anyway, the captain on the sea vessel Endeavor was Captain Cook."

Manny interrupted, "Captain Hook? The Captain Hook?"

"No, not Captain Hook, Captain Cook. Captain Hook doesn't have anything to do with the space program. Captain Hook hunts Peter Pan, not rockets. Captain Cook discovered Hawaii. And then a lot of the Hawaiians got small pox from Cook and his crew and they died."

"I'm confused," Manny said. I shook my head in agreement.

"Okay, listen closely," Eddie said. "Captain James Cook was the captain of a ship and the space shuttle was named after that ship. The ship's name was Endeavor."

"Cool," Manny said. "I should have written mine about space."

"Oh my gosh, you guys. The word endeavor means a big mission or goal," Marina explained.

"That's probably why they named the rocket Endeavor, because it was on a big mission," I added.

"No, I'm telling you it was named after a ship," Eddie said.

"Okay, enough talk about rockets and ships. Josh, let's hear yours." Marina sighed.

"Okay," I said and grinned.

Who cut the cheese, I really must know?
The ham sandwich is ready to go.

"That's funny," Manny laughed.
"Funny in an immature sort of way," Marina said.

"Thanks, I think," I answered. I couldn't tell if that was a compliment or a cut down. It was always like that with Marina.

"Ham and cheese sounds good," was all Eddie said.

"Your turn Eddie," Marina said in a bossy tone.

"Okay, here it goes," Eddie mumbled.

Roses are red and Josh likes pink
I think Ms. Waverly is really neat.

Marina giggled.

"Something funny?" Eddie said.

"Uh, no," she said. "But it doesn't rhyme."

"What part?" he asked.

"The part that's supposed to rhyme," she snapped.

"Like I said, what part?"

"Pink and neat don't rhyme," Marina said getting very frustrated.

Eddie asked, "What rhymes with pink then?"

"Stink," I answered trying to get him back for the "Josh likes pink" line.

"Hey, thanks, Josh," Eddie said as he erased the old line and scribbled a new one. "How 'bout this?"

Roses are red and Josh likes pink
Ms. Waverly's perfume doesn't stink.

"That works better," Marina said.

"Thanks," Eddie said to Marina but looked right at me when he said it.

I could tell by his grin he thought he was going to win. Great, now I was rhyming in my head. I couldn't wait until this poetry unit was over.

Oh no, that rumbling feeling was back. I could feel another fart coming on. *POOF!* Another silent but deadly slipped out.

Manny grabbed his nose and gagged.

Marina pulled her shirt over her nose. "Come on, Eddie, enough."

"That wasn't me that time. Actually, it wasn't me the last time either," Eddie said, looking in my direction.

I felt my face turn beet red, even redder than that stupid fake apple on Ms. Waverly's desk. My color gave me away.

"Why, Josh, why?" Manny asked.

By now the smell had traveled to the next table group. They laughed and held their noses. Eddie laughed the hardest. He knew my fart didn't count because it was silent. It had to be *loud* and *stinky* to qualify for the bet.

Now the smell had traveled around the entire room. The whole class was holding their noses and giggling.

"What's the problem?" Ms. Waverly said as she hovered over our group. Somehow she always knew where the trouble started.

Everyone stopped their laughter.

"No problem," Marina said.

Ms. Waverly nodded. Just then she got a strong whiff of the problem. Then I saw her do something I'd never seen a teacher do. She covered her mouth and nose. She tried to make it look like she was just thinking, but we all knew she was trying not to smell.

Then, another SBD slipped and the smell hit the class instantly. They all roared with laughter. Ms. Waverly pointed to the windows and Eddie stood up and went over to open them. This made the class laugh even harder.

*   *   *

Ms. Behr reached over to the air freshener and turned the dial all the way up. It was no use. It couldn't mask the SBD's I'd been letting during our counseling session. Every time Eddie got a whiff, he cracked up laughing. Eddie had one of those laughs that was infectious. When you heard it, you had to laugh too. Actually, you couldn't really hear his laugh at all. Eddie just kind of shook all over with his mouth open and no sound came out. It was hilarious. And when he laughed really hard, he cried. He had tears streaming down his face right now. I was wiping tears from my eyes also. Not because I was laughing, which I was, but because the air freshener was so strong.

My biggest problem at the moment was that when I laughed real hard, more farts snuck out. The office was one big smell-fest. Ms. Behr opened the door to let in some fresh air. Too bad there wasn't a window in her small office.

"Boys, pull yourselves together," she scolded. "Honestly, it's just a little gas, it happens to everyone. Now, does one of you need to use the bathroom?"

This made us laugh even harder. Ms. Behr just shook her head.

"Well, we've wasted too much time. Let's call it a day. I'll see you boys later this week," she said and scooted us out of her office.

As we hurried out to what was left of our recess, I heard Ms. Behr say under her breath, "Well, at least they're not fighting."

I also noticed she didn't go back into her office. Instead, she headed to the teacher's lounge. Good move, it was pretty ripe in there.

CHAPTER 9

The creamy oatmeal with sliced bananas was comforting. It slid down my throat and warmed my tummy. According to the internet, bananas, veggies, and foods high in fiber like oatmeal can sometimes cause gas. I decided to give it a try this Tuesday morning.

"Oatmeal today, huh, Josh. I hate oatmeal," Eddie said as he ate his Cheerios.

"Cheerios are made from oats," I said.

"Whatever, nerd king."

"No, really. Look on the box."

Eddie read the box and laughed. "Oh yeah, it says it's made from oats. I guess I do like oatmeal, just not the mushy oatmeal. I like it pressed into little round donut shapes. I also like donuts. That must be why I like Cheerios." Eddie took a huge spoonful and slurped it up.

I couldn't follow Eddie's thinking. It was weird how he could be so smart about certain things and so clueless about others. That must be why he didn't do well in school. Lately, I noticed something really interesting about Eddie. If he watched a show on TV, he remembered everything about it. It was like all the information got stuck in his brain forever. But if he read something, he forgot it almost instantly. I wondered if I should mention it to my dad or Allie or even Ms. Waverly.

"Here's your healthy lunch," Allie said and handed me my lunch bag. She handed one to Eddie also.

"Thanks."

"I'm glad to see you eating healthy. I packed carrots, celery and orange slices, just like you asked. I also threw in a sandwich, too." Allie handed a second bag to Eddie. "I packed the same for you."

"What? Only one sandwich. Come on, mom. I need at least two." Eddie said.

"Eddie, I don't know if you noticed or not but you are losing weight and I don't think you need two sandwiches anymore," Allie said.

I looked at Eddie; he did seem to be shrinking around the middle. Maybe it was because he wasn't eating all those cookies and junk he used to take from our classmates on the bus.

"Fine. One sandwich, but couldn't you put in some chips?" Eddie asked.

"A few carrots and orange slices never hurt anyone," Allie laughed and went back into the kitchen.

"Look on the bright side, Eddie. At least we won't get scurvy," I added.

"That's pretty funny," Eddie said and chased me out of the dining room.

*   *   *

When we came back to our classroom after lunch, this was written on the board.

Pink cherry blossoms
Sweet-scented, lovely petals
Spring time has arrived

"This is an example of a Haiku. It is a Japanese poem. Usually it focuses on a season or time of year. You will notice that the first line has five syllables, the second line has seven and the third line has five again. It does not have to rhyme," Ms. Waverly said. "Please break up into your groups and begin working on your Haikus."

We got up and moved to our stations.

"We should each take a different season. Then maybe Ms. Waverly will put ours up on the poetry board," Marina said.

Ms. Waverly created a special bulletin board just for our poems. She said she would pick four or five really good poems each day. Whoever she picked got to read their poem in front of the class. Marina read hers yesterday. Eddie's didn't get picked yesterday. Thank goodness.

"You already have one poem up there," Manny said.

"True, but I love writing and I'm good at it so I should get one poem up there each day," she said.

"Yeah, you should really try to do that," I said secretly thinking it would limit Eddie's chances if Marina got one up each day. If Eddie didn't read his in front of the class, he would lose the bet.

"Thanks, Josh. Now, I'll take winter and Manny you can have summer. Josh can take spring and Eddie will take fall," she said in a bossy tone.

"I'm already working on spring, so buzz off," Eddie grumbled as he worked on his Haiku.

"Fine, then Josh can take fall." she pouted. She wasn't about to cross Eddie.

"Sure," I said. Normally I would have told her to quit being so bossy, but I needed her as an ally. We spent the next fifteen minutes writing and counting syllables on our hands. Finally we were ready to share.

"Who wants to go first?" Manny asked.

I thought Marina would raise her hand but she was kind of quiet. Maybe Eddie had hurt her feelings.

"I'll go," I said.

Fall is here today
Leaves starting to fall away
Fall, fall, fall, fall, fall.

"That's good," Manny said.

Marina snorted.

"What's wrong with it?" I asked her.

"Well, first of all, Ms. Waverly said that it didn't have to rhyme," she said.

"She didn't say it couldn't rhyme." Manny came to my defense.

She continued on as if Manny hadn't said anything. "And the last line just repeats the same word five times."

"I'm good with that," I answered.

She just rolled her eyes. "Why don't you go next Manny."

"Okay," he said nervously.

Now it's summertime
Let's swim in the pool all day
Splash, splash, splash, splash, splash

"I really like it!" I said.

"Come on. It has the exact same problem as yours does," Marina sighed.

"That's why I like it," I added.

"It just repeats the word splash five times."

"Why don't you help him fix it instead of being so bossy? Since you're so good at writing and all," Eddie said. For a moment, the old Eddie was back.

Marina looked a little stunned. That was the second time Eddie had put her in her place. She blinked a few times and looked away for a moment. Her eyes seemed a little teary. Maybe she didn't know she was bossy. Or maybe she didn't realize how hard school was for Eddie.

"Actually, it's not bad, Manny. But I do have a suggestion if you would like to make it better," she said apologetically.

"Sure," Manny said. Nothing ruffled Manny's feathers. He was good-natured.

"Maybe you could add some different words on the last line that described swimming," she said.

"Yeah, like dive," I added.

"Or cannonball!" Eddie piped in.

Manny scribbled furiously at the suggestions. I decided to take Marina's advice too and I changed some of my words. In the end here's how our Haikus changed:

> *Now it's summertime*
> *Let's swim in the pool all day*
> *Splash, dive, cannonball!*

> *Fall is here today*
> *Leaves starting to fall away*
> *Fall, drop, swoosh, slide, fall.*

We all agreed they both sounded better even though mine still had two falls in it.

"I'll go now," Marina said and then added, "Unless you want to go next Eddie."

"Naw, go ahead," he said.

> *Brittle, delicate*
> *Icy, translucent beauty*
> *Winter icicle*

"That was great," I said.

"What's translucent?" Manny asked.

"It means you can see light through something but can't see through it perfectly," she answered.

"Oh, I get it. When you look through an icicle, everything looks kind of white and funny." Manny said. Marina finally smiled.

"My turn," Eddie said gruffly.

> *Spring flowers are not*
> *As beautiful as Ms. Wav-*
> *erly my teacher*

"You like Ms. Waverly?" Manny asked.

"Yeah, she's my favorite teacher. You got a problem with that?" Eddie asked.

"No, she's nice. No problem," Manny back-peddled.

"Can I make a suggestion?" Marina pried cautiously.

"Suit yourself," Eddie answered.

It's not bad, it's just a little confusing where you break Ms. Waverly's name up onto two different lines."

"Yeah, it stinks. I know," Eddie said.

"When you write poetry, it's like you are expressing yourself. What else do you like? I mean besides Ms. Waverly?" she said as a small grin played around the corners of her mouth.

"I guess I like Halloween. Last year I went as the Swamp Ape," he answered.

"What's a Swamp Ape?" she said.

Wow, Marina didn't know something.

"It's kind of like Bigfoot but he lives in the Everglades in Florida. Oh yeah, and he really stinks. Sometimes he's called the Skunk Ape," he added.

"Is that why you smelled last year at Halloween?" I asked remembering how Eddie reeked when I passed by him while trick or treating. Well, not so much as passed by as when he knocked me into the bushes and took most of my candy.

"No, the costume was just really hot and I forgot to wear deodorant."

"Yeah, you did stink," Manny said, forgetting who he was talking, too. "But it was a cool costume. All big and hairy. I didn't know it was the Swamp Ape. I thought you were Bigfoot."

"That's a common mistake. Many people confuse the Swamp Ape for Bigfoot, or 'Sasquatch' as Native Americans call him. Some people also confuse him with the Abominable Snowman or 'Yeti' as he is

80

known in the Himalayans. Rumor has it, that if you shoot at the Swamp Ape, you'll find scales under his fur," Eddie said.

"How do you know all that?" Manny asked in wonder.

"I learned about it when I was watching a show called *Bigfoot, the Abominable Snowman and the Swamp Ape*. It was pretty good."

"Maybe you should write about that," Marina suggested.

"Okay," Eddie said and began writing enthusiastically.

Marina and Manny went to turn in their poems.

"Don't forget the bet," I whispered to Eddie. I didn't want him to win but I knew he couldn't put all that and a love letter to Ms. Waverly in the same Haiku. I needed him to fail.

Marina and Manny returned. Eddie declared his Haiku complete.

"Here it goes," he announced.

> *Things I think are great*
> *Big Foot, Yeti, the Swamp Ape*
> *And Ms. Waverly*

"I even got it to rhyme." Eddie smiled to himself.

"Wow, that's better than Marina's," Manny said.

Marina looked shocked. I was devastated. I didn't think he could pull it off. I was wrong. Come to think of it, I'd noticed I'd been wrong more than right when it came to Eddie. I had to increase my game.

Eddie or the Swamp Ape?

While I munched happily on carrots and celery sticks, I realized that lunchtime was more fun when Eddie sat at our table. I watched Eddie look down at his orange slices and knew he wouldn't be able to eat them like a normal person.

Eddie stuck an orange wedge in his mouth and pretended to be a monster. He went from table to table growling at everyone until a lunchroom monitor told him to go sit down. Too late, everyone was already laughing, including me.

"What's that?" Paul asked when he looked at my sandwich.

I unwrapped the sandwich and surveyed it. "It looks like alfalfa sprouts, cucumbers, tomatoes and some kind of white cheese on wheat bread. It's really healthy," I told him. Wow, Allie really went overboard.

"It doesn't look that good to me," Paul said as he bit into his peanut butter and jelly sandwich.

"For your information, it is delicious," I answered and took a bite. I tried to keep a smile on my face because the sandwich was awful. Although I didn't care, I just wanted it to work its magic. I looked at Eddie to see if he liked the sandwich.

I watched Eddie bite into a salami and cheese sandwich on Italian bread. Then he swallowed hard and picked up another sandwich, this time it was a bologna and cheese sandwich and he took an even bigger bite.

"Where'd you get those sandwiches?" I asked. My question was answered when I saw Chelsea and Marina splitting the sandwich Allie had made for Eddie.

"What? It looked good," Chelsea said.

"Yeah, like a salad on bread," Marina said.

"It's not bad, especially after we put some ranch dressing on it," Chelsea added.

I quickly grabbed a few ranch packets from the salad bar and smothered my sandwich. It tasted much better. Then out of the blue, it happened. A glorious fart to be heard throughout the cafetorium. This time I wasn't embarrassed, I was excited. I had won my portion of the bet!

The entire cafetorium burst into laughter. All eyes were on me.

"Josh, why?" Chelsea asked.

I shrugged my shoulders like I didn't know why.

"Awesome!" Paul said.

Several teachers gave me dirty looks, but I saw a few of them laughing, too.

After the craziness had died down, I leaned over to Eddie. "So, what do you think?"

"I think that's the loudest fart I've ever heard. Even louder than Carter the Farter's famous farts," Eddie said.

I couldn't help but beam with a little pride. Last year Carter the Farter gave Eddie a run for his money for the best farter in school. "Thanks," I said.

"Wait, I didn't finish. I meant to say that was the loudest fart I've heard that didn't smell." Eddie smirked.

Oh, no! He was right. It didn't smell. It was just really loud. It had to be loud and smelly for me to win. I was upset and that wasn't the worst part. I felt another coming on.

BBBRRRROOUT!!! Great, loud with no smell! Chelsea and Marina were staring at me with their mouths open.

"Maybe it was the sandwich," I told them sheepishly.

They both pushed Allie's homemade sandwich away. I've never heard so much laughing in my life.

CHAPTER 10

On Wednesday morning, I knew if I combined the foods I had eaten in the last two days I would have the perfect farting combination. My dad made me oatmeal and eggs. The eggs would provide the smell and the oatmeal the fiber.

"Oatmeal and eggs. Weird breakfast," Eddie said as he ate a bowl of Cheerios and a plate of eggs.

"It's the same thing you're having," I said impatiently.

"Ah, no it isn't. I'm having cereal and eggs," Eddie said. I guess he forgot that Cheerios were made of oats. That didn't take long.

"Hey Allie," I called from the table. "Can I have another lunch like yesterday? Except maybe a little ham on my sandwich? Pretty please?"

"No problem, I'll pack one for you too Eddie." she said.

"Hey, mom. That sandwich was great but maybe you could leave off the alfalfa sprouts this time?"

"Okay, dear," Allie replied.

"And maybe leave off the cucumbers and tomatoes and lettuce."

"So you just want a ham sandwich," she asked.

"No, you can put cheese on it," Eddie said.

"So, you want a plain ham and cheese sandwich. Is that it?"

"Perfect." Eddie look relieved.

*   *   *

When we walked into class this morning there were three words written in big letters on the white board: Heart, Eagle, and Mountain. I had a feeling this had something to do with our next poetry assignment.

Ms. Waverly drew a heart next to the word heart. It was a little lopsided. She tried to draw an eagle next to the word eagle, but it looked more like a turkey or vulture. "Okay class, as you can see today our poems will have a theme."

I was right. I knew it was about poetry.

Ms. Waverly erased the vulture-like bird and started over. Now her eagle looked like a scary penguin. There was a sprinkling of laughter throughout the room. She erased the penguin and gave a loud sigh.

"Ms. Waverly," Eddie said.

"Yes, Eddie?"

"If you want, I can draw an eagle for you." The room grew quiet. Eddie never volunteered in class.

Ms. Waverly looked relieved. "Yes, please, Eddie. Come up here and draw an eagle."

Eddie strutted his way up to the board and proceeded to draw an eagle. "See Ms. Waverly, you just gotta draw a small oval for the head and a larger oval for the body," Eddie said as he drew with the marker.

"Then draw a neck between the head and body to connect it together."

Eddie was on a roll. It was really fun to watch him draw. Every line he drew fit perfectly into the next.

"Then you have to draw a beak. Of course everyone knows that an eagle's beak turns down at the tip," he said as he sketched.

It was true. An eagle's beak did turn down at the tip. I'd never noticed before.

"Then add a few wings, and a tail and you're done."

We all looked at the eagle in amazement, but no one more so than Ms. Waverly. Paul started clapping his hands and soon everyone joined in, including Ms. Waverly.

"My Eddie, I had no idea how well you could draw. Did you visualize an eagle before your drew it?"

"Um, I have a really cool poster of an eagle. I just thought back to what that poster looked like."

"That's astonishing. Very good, Eddie. Would you like to draw some mountains next to the word mountain?" she asked.

"Sure." Eddie went back to drawing on the board. The mountain wasn't as impressive as the eagle, but I bet it was better than what anyone else could draw. Most kids would just draw an upside down letter V for a mountain, but not Eddie. He drew a whole mountain range. And the mountains looked real, too. They had lumps and bumps and overlapped each other. He even drew the tops of the mountains covered in snow. I bet Mr. Cutler, our art teacher, couldn't draw mountains that good.

"Thank you, Eddie. You can go back to your seat. Actually class, please get into your poetry groups. This assignment today is called free verse."

Ms. Waverly stopped talking while we moved our desks and got into our poetry stations. Once we were all settled she started up again.

"This poem will be the most fun to write," she said.

Manny rolled his eyes at me. I agreed.

Ms. Waverly explained we were to create our free verse by listing words that fit with the symbols we chose. Manny and I picked the awesome eagle Eddie drew. Marina picked the mountain, and of course, Eddie had to pick the heart for Ms. Waverly.

"I think I will make my poem more metaphoric than realistic," Marina told us.

"What?" Manny said.

Marina rolled her eyes at all of us. She must be getting sick of sitting next to us and having to explain everything she said.

"I mean, I'm going to write about a mountain but not really about a mountain."

None of us understood that. She huffed like a girl and lowered her head to work on her poem. I couldn't swear but I think I heard her mumble, "Idiots".

"Now class, since I expect at least four lines of free verse, these poems won't be due until Friday. You will not have time to work on them tomorrow because of our scheduled field trip," Ms. Waverly said.

Eddie raised his hand.

"Yes, Eddie?"

"Will we have time on Friday to read our poems? Because if not I could quickly finish this now and read it today."

"Well, I certainly appreciate your enthusiasm but I want you all to take your time with this assignment. So no poems will be read today. They can be read on Friday. Plus, I really want to see the connection between your words and the symbols on the board," Ms. Waverly said.

Eddie's hand slowly went down. He looked crushed. But then he looked at me and said, "I can do this."

Manny said, "Josh didn't say you couldn't."

"Yeah, maybe not out loud but he was thinking it." Eddie said.

Eddie was right, I was thinking it. *How did he know?*

Marina looked up from her paper. "Eddie, it's not so bad if you start like Ms. Waverly said and make a list of words that you think of when you see a heart."

"Right, I can do this," Eddie said again and began writing.

Manny and I decided to combine our list of words since we were both doing eagles. It was easier when we worked together.

After about fifteen minutes Ms. Waverly told us to share our words with our group. Eddie went first.

"I wrote down human organ, blood, blood vessels, pumping, valves, transplant…"

"Hold up. Those are very good words and very graphic. Do you have any words that aren't so scientific?" Marina asked.

"Um, yeah." Eddie looked to the bottom of his page. "I have deck of cards, cobwebs, spiders…"

"Wait. How do they remind you of a heart?" Manny said. I kept quiet. There was no way Eddie was going to get his poem read on Friday.

"Before my parents split up, we used to play a card game called Hearts. It was really fun. I won most of the time."

I didn't know that about Eddie. He rarely talked about things he did when his parents were together.

"I've heard of that game," Marina said. "It does sound fun."

"Okay, so deck of cards makes sense but what about spiders and cobwebs?" Manny asked.

"There was this one time when I was outside near the back fence of my old house. I was hunting for dinosaur bones."

All of our eyes got wide. "Did you find one?" I couldn't help but ask.

"That's a completely different story." Eddie cleared his throat. "Now while I had my head down looking for footprints, fossils, anything to do with a dinosaur, I felt the hair on my neck stand up. I mean I felt like there was something there, something ready to get me. I was afraid to look up."

We all held our breath. We were hanging on every word. Eddie sure could tell a story.

"I slowly raised my head. Staring me straight in the eyes was the biggest spider I'd ever seen. I froze. It was looking at me as if I were lunch. I knew it could eat me if it wanted to, it was that big."

"What'd you do?" Manny whispered.

"I did what any good dinosaur hunter would do. I jumped back fast, really fast. Easily four or five feet in one quick movement. That's when I noticed it. The spider's cobweb was in the shape of a huge heart.

It was one of the most incredible things I'd ever seen. I tried to get my mom to come and see it but she hates spiders and was worried it could be poisonous. So I had to admire it alone. The next day I went to see it and it was gone."

"Good story, I see why you picked those words. Maybe you could find some way to use them in your poem," Marina said.

"Yeah, use them. Most people think of Valentine's Day when they see a heart but cobwebs are so much better," I said, knowing that no one but the three of us would understand his poem, especially Ms. Waverly.

"Valentine's Day! That's a great idea. I never even thought of that. Thanks, Josh." Eddie added Valentine's Day to his list of words.

Me and my great, big mouth.

*   *   *

The raindrops slipped down the cafetorium windowpane. Nothing was worse than rain on PE day. Coach Fox reached into the closet and pulled the parachute out. The parachute! Probably the funnest thing to do in PE ever! Nothing was better than rain on PE day.

Coach Fox unfurled the parachute to the squeals and delights of the entire class. We all stood around it and grabbed an edge. It felt silky smooth even though it was a bit tattered and frayed from years of use but we didn't care. We all loved it.

Coach Fox had us warm-up by making waves. First she told us to make little waves by moving our hands and wrists. Next, we made big waves by moving our entire arms. Then Coach Fox placed a ball of yarn on the parachute and we had to keep making waves until the yarn unrolled. It was taking forever, but it was fun. The hardest part was trying to keep it from going through the hole in the middle.

While we were playing, I felt the pressure start to build in my intestines. I knew I could let a world class fart in PE.

"Hey, Eddie," I yelled over our shrieking classmates, "Does it count if I let a fart in front of Coach Fox? She's our teacher just not our classroom teacher."

"Yeah, it's cool. I don't care. Whatever," was all he said.

I noticed that Eddie had been getting a little nicer lately. I didn't know why. I wondered if it was because he was finding out that when he was nice to people, they were nicer to him. Come to think of it, he was actually doing better in school too. Weird.

"Now, it's time for Under the Mountain!" Coach Fox announced.

The entire class burst in cheers. Under the Mountain was the best part of parachute day. These were the rules: Everyone fluffs the parachute really high into the air. Then, as it's floating down you grabbed the edge and tucked it under your bottom and sit down really fast. It's so cool because every kid can see everyone else under the parachute mountain. Then the parachute drifts down and covers us all.

"Here we go!" Coach Fox said, and blew her whistle. At the exact same moment I let a fart that would put a band of trumpets to shame. The problem was that no one heard it because of the whistle.

Kids screamed and laughed and tucked the parachute under their bottoms. We were all engulfed in a sea of color but, oh the smell! My fart was world class, even out doing Eddie's in raunchiness and odor. My poor classmates were trapped Under the Smelly Mountain!

As the fart progressed around the dome, kids scrambled for the little hole in the middle of the chute, just to get a whiff of fresh air. I couldn't figure out why they just didn't step out from under the parachute. It would have been easier. Maybe the odor was somehow fogging up their brains.

Chaos was abundant as kids tripped over each other and clawed their way to the little hole. I could see Eddie laughing his pants off. The parachute drifted over the entire class and body parts became tangled. It took Coach Fox five minutes to free us all and another five minutes to find out what had happened. Of course, I was much too cowardly to admit to the fart. Plus, no one heard it so it didn't count. Only Eddie knew and he didn't even rat me out. How odd. I guess parachute day wasn't so fun after all.

CHAPTER 11

What was going on? It was Thursday and Eddie was sprawled out in the back seat of the school bus as usual but this time he wasn't alone. Everyone knew he always sat in the back and normally no one dared to sit back there next to him. But today it was different. Everyone seemed to want to hang out in the back of the bus. I bet it was because Ms. Waverly was on board on account of our field trip. Kids knew Eddie wouldn't do anything wrong in front of her. That had to be it. Didn't it?

"So then I challenged him to a spit off," Eddie said.

"Ew, what's that?" Chelsea asked.

"That's when both guys spit and whoever spits the farthest wins," Paul answered.

"Yes, but also if you can make your spit bounce you are the winner even if it doesn't go as far as the other guy's does," Manny added.

"Spit doesn't bounce," Marina said.

"Ah, yeah it does if it has enough snottiness to it. Everyone knows that," Eddie said annoyed.

"You guys are gross," Marina said but continued to listen to the story.

"So who won?" Chelsea asked.

"I did of course. It was a double victory because I spit the farthest and it bounced." Eddie beamed.

A horrible, sulfuric smell hung in the air. And for once it wasn't me. Yep, we'd arrived at our field trip destination spot: the water treatment plant.

Ms. Waverly stood at the front of the bus. "Listen up. You kids are in for a real treat. You get to see first hand how the water we use everyday gets cleaned and purified so we may use it again."

"What's that smell?" Marina asked.

"I think Josh just let one," Eddie added too low for Ms. Waverly to hear but loud enough for everyone in the back of the bus to hear. The back of the bus erupted in laughter until Ms. Waverly gave us the freeze eye.

My face turned as pink as the stupid swirl on my skateboard. I was starting to get the reputation of being a farter. *How would I ever live that down?* And I hadn't even completed the dare yet. I reached into my jacket and patted my secret weapon. It was a small zip-lock bag full of chopped broccoli. Oh yes, I found the ultimate fart food and I'd brought it along for the ride. It's amazing the information you can find on the internet. Broccoli topped the list time after time when I searched for the foods that cause the loudest and smelliest farts.

We exited the bus and began our tour. A small, round lady with bright red glasses was waiting for our class. Her hair matched her glasses. I wondered if she planned it that way.

"Hi everyone, my name is Jan and you can call me Jan," she said. Ms. Waverly snickered a bit but there was no response from anyone else.

"That usually gets a laugh," Jan said.

A few kids laughed, but I think it was just so she wouldn't feel bad. We were in for a long day with lame jokes like that.

"Okay, that's a little better. Everyone follow me to our first exciting stop."

We all obeyed. As we walked, I popped a piece of broccoli in my mouth.

"Here we have the pit." Jan said pointing to the large in-ground concrete pool of sludgy, slimy water. "The waste water from your house flows through that pipe. The pit filters out the garbage."

We all peered over the edge to look.

"I can see a popsicle stick," Paul said.

"I see a plastic bag," Marina added.

Suddenly I let out a tremendous fart. It was loud like a brass horn, but the sound of rushing water was so loud only the person next to me heard it. And that someone was Eddie, of course. It was PE all over again.

"Josh, you really stink at farting," Eddie laughed.

"What do you mean? That was perfect!" I argued.

"Only I heard it. You have to plan better. You can't just let one rip at any time. You're wasting farts."

"Well, I can't hold them in. If they want to come out, I can't stop them."

"Amateur." Eddie shrugged.

Jan led us to the next stop in what was easily the most boring field trip ever. "This is the settling tank," Jan said.

It was another big, concrete, rectangular tank set into the ground. It smelled horrible. I thought Eddie's farts were bad but the settling tank really reeked.

"Any questions?" Jan asked.

"What's all the icky stuff floating on the top?" Chelsea asked.

"That's grease and scum. Straight from your home I might add," Jan said.

"Ew," was all Chelsea said.

"Why does it stink so bad?" Manny asked.

"It is raw sewage from your toilets," Jan answered.

This got a giant "Ew" from the group and Jan laughed, "Well, it has to go someplace."

BAM-BAM-BAM!! Three very loud farts exploded from my behind. They were superb! Finally, I had won my side of the bet. Everyone turned to stare, even Jan and Ms. Waverly.

The entire class busted a gut laughing. Ms. Waverly and Jan covered their mouths to try to hide the fact that they were laughing, too. It didn't work. I could tell. Eddie was laughing the hardest. Everyone was holding their noses, too. Let them hold their noses! I had won the fart bet! Never mind that my face was a very deep shade of red from embarrassment.

It took forever for the mayhem to die down, but finally it did. We continued our tour through the water treatment plant. Eddie could not stop laughing. Even five minutes later he was still wiping tears from his eyes.

"What's so funny, Eddie? It was just a fart. Everyone else has forgotten it," I snapped. "I'd think that you'd be more concerned I'd just completed my dare."

That made him laugh even harder and more tears squirted out of his eyes. "Josh, that was classic. People will be talking about that fart for years!"

"Thanks, I think," I answered. I wasn't sure I wanted that memory to live on forever in the minds of my classmates.

"Too bad you couldn't smell it," Eddie added.

"What? Didn't you see everyone holding their noses? Of course you could smell it!" I added but then had a sinking feeling in my gut. Eddie was right. Everyone had been holding their noses before the fart because of the settling tank smell. I just embarrassed myself for nothing.

"You really do stink at farting," Eddie said with a smile.

*   *   *

I popped the straw in my grape juice box and sucked up the sweet drink. I looked at the lake in front of me and felt the cool fall breeze on my face. This was hands down the best part of the field trip. We were eating lunch at a park next to our local aquifer. The aquifer was a big lake that supplied all the water for our town. There was something really great about eating lunch outside on a school day, especially when sitting on the grass. It made you feel free.

I took a huge bite of my PB&J. Jelly stuck to the side of my mouth and I licked it off. Strawberry. Yummy.

Everyone was quiet and soaking up the sun when Eddie started in, "Did I tell you guys I'm getting my own room?" he said to our regular lunch crowd.

"Cool," Paul answered. "Can I come over and see it?"

*Did Paul just ask Eddie if he could come over? What was going on? Paul was my friend, not Eddie's. And did Eddie say **his** new room?*

"Me too," Manny added.

Now Manny too?

"Anyway, it's really awesome. The ceiling is super tall like a church, but it feels more like you're in a log cabin because it's covered with wood. There's enough room for two beds. One for me and one for anyone who wants to stay over night," Eddie continued.

"I do," Paul and Manny said at the same time.

"Okay, but it's not finished yet. The walls still have to be painted and some other junk. But maybe this weekend you guys can sleep over."

"Sweet," Manny said.

"Yeah, sweet," Paul added.

Even as I sat next to my two best friends, I felt all alone. I had to win that room. I popped some more broccoli in my mouth. Eddie eyed me and an evil grin played across his lips. He thought he'd already won and he hadn't even completed his dare yet. He only had one day left. *Where did he get his confidence? I wish I had it.*

*   *   *

Every child can recall a moment of great embarrassment in their life which they will remember forever. Mine happened that afternoon on the bus as we pulled back into our school after the field trip. Ms. Waverly was a stickler for leaving a bus spotless. Each kid had to pick up three pieces of garbage off the bus floor before we could exit.

"Josh, please come up here and get the bag," Ms. Waverly commanded.

I walked to the front of the bus and retrieved the plastic bag that would house all the garbage we collected.

"Please start at the back and make your way forward," she said, but we all knew the drill.

Each kid was supposed to put their garbage in the bag and then get in line. That way, when the bag kid got to the door, the entire bus would be clean and we'd be in a straight line, ready to exit. I hated being the bag kid. Why did Ms. Waverly always have to be so thorough?

I schlepped my way to the back of the bus and held the bag out for Eddie, Manny and Paul. They threw their garbage in it and got in line behind me. The next step I took was magnificent and shameful at the same time. Raaaaat! I let out a nice loud fart that smelled wonderfully horrible. Not everyone heard it though; kids on buses do tend to be loud.

"Dude," Paul said and grabbed his nose.

Manny and Eddie laughed.

Marina and Chelsea deposited their garbage into the bag with one hand and held their noses with the other.

Each step I took produced another loud and smelly fart. Rat-ta-tat-tat! One right after the other.

"Nice machine gun!" Matthew laughed as I held the bag out for his garbage.

The farts did sound like a machine gun. My classmates were caught in the line of fire behind me. They were forced to smell the horror. There was no escape. I tried to move quicker, but the farts just came quicker. Rat-tat-tat! Rat-tat-tat!

Kids were either howling with laughter or holding their noses. Some were even fanning the air. It was no use. The smell was just too powerful. A couple of kids stuck their heads out the window until Ms. Waverly made them put the windows back up. She believed in leaving the bus the way we found it. By the time I'd gotten to the front of the bus, everyone including Ms. Waverly had heard my toots and gotten a whiff. I'd won my part of the bet, but at the expense of my self-esteem.

CHAPTER 12

Since I had won my dare yesterday, the only thing that had me worried today was our poetry session. Even though Ms. Waverly told us we would have time to finish our free verse poem in class, I noticed that Eddie was working on his last night. He was really serious about winning his dare. Probably because he already told Paul and Manny about the super cool attic room. He was even quiet at breakfast.

"Everyone please get into your poetry groups," Ms. Waverly told us.

Manny and I still had a lot to do, so we got right down to business.

"I finished mine already," Marina informed us. "Does anyone want some help?"

Before Manny or I could utter a yes, Eddie scooted his chair closer to Marina. "Yeah, I really want it to be good so I can read it in front of the class today."

Marina looked a little skeptical but decided to help him anyway. I couldn't spy on him because Manny

103

and I still had to finish our poems. I didn't want to ruin my "A" average.

"How 'bout I change some of the words so our poems aren't completely identical," Manny suggested.

"That's probably a good idea. Our poems are sounding similar," I said.

"Okay, what's your first line?" Manny asked.

"Flying high with wings real big," I said.

"Right. Mine will say: Flying low with wings spread out."

"Good. That's not even close. This should be easy," I said.

"What's your next line?" Manny asked.

"How about: Over a field of corn."

"I'll change mine to: It lands in a rice field."

"Do you think we should both use the word field?" I asked.

"I don't see the problem. What else are eagles supposed to fly over?"

"Good point. Let's keep going."

Ms. Waverly broke our concentration. "Now, I want everyone to read their poem to their group and decide who has the best description of their symbol. That student will read theirs in front of the class.

Marina decided to go first.

MOUNTAIN
Writing a story is like climbing a mountain.
My story starts small
One paragraph, then two
Soon it is a whole page
Pages turn into chapters
Chapters turn into a book
The top of the mountain.

"Wow," I said.

"I don't get it, but I like it," Manny said.

"Not bad," Eddie added. "But I thought you were going to write about a real mountain."

"No, I wanted to show my inner feelings," she said.

"Okay then, good job," Eddie said although he looked a little confused.

"Thanks."

I can't believe Eddie complimented her poem. I mean it wasn't that good. I didn't even picture a mountain when she read it. Wasn't that the whole purpose of this assignment?

"I'll go next," I volunteered.

EAGLE

Flying high with wings real big
Over a field of corn
The eagle dives down to grab a mouse
It must be lunchtime.

"Really good Josh. I could visualize the eagle," Marina said.

Now that's what I'm talking about!

"My turn," Manny said.

EAGLE

Flying low with wings spread out
The eagle lands in a rice field
A little mouse runs fast
It doesn't want to be lunch.

Nobody said a word until Eddie started laughing. "It's almost exactly the same as Josh's."

"So?" I said. "I think they're both good."

Marina was trying to stifle her laughter. "Yeah, they're both good. But Eddie has a point. They are very similar."

"That's because we worked on them together," Manny said.

"I know, but I wouldn't know how to choose between them," Marina said.

"I would like to read mine in front of the class today. Does anyone have an objection?" Eddie asked.

"Wait. We haven't even heard yours yet. And Marina's was really good." I said. I didn't want our group to vote for Eddie's poem.

"I've already read a couple of mine. I think it is only fair to let one of you guys read today. Plus I don't think anyone will get the meaning of mine judging by Manny's and Eddie's reactions," Marina said.

"Well, then I vote for Manny," I said.

"Hey, we haven't heard Eddie's yet and I really don't want to get up in front of the class," Manny said. "I vote for Eddie."

"I second it," Marina said.

"I third it." Eddie smiled. "Looks like you're out-voted Josh. I'm the winner today."

"Not so fast, Eddie. Remember the poem has to be a love poem to… I mean it has to describe a heart." Oops, I almost lost the bet by saying Eddie's dare in front of Manny and Marina.

"Don't worry, it does." Eddie smiled.

My stomach was beginning to hurt. I don't know if it was all that broccoli I ate yesterday or the fact that my group just voted for Eddie to read his poem.

Either way, I felt like doubling over. I thought about asking to use the restroom, but I was afraid I would miss Eddie recite his love poem. And if I knew Eddie, it was going to be a big production. He never did anything small.

* * *

"And now for our last group. Who will be reading today?" Ms. Waverly asked our group.

Eddie raised his hand. I could see he was a bit nervous. His hand was shaking slightly. He didn't look in my direction at all.

"Eddie, what a surprise. Wonderful. Come up to the front, please."

Eddie trudged up to the front of the class. He had a very serious expression on his face. It almost made him look menacing.

"My poem is…" Eddie stopped to clear his throat. He covered his mouth with his fist and made a coughing noise again to clear his throat. I think he was stalling for time.

"Eddie, do you need to get a drink of water?" Ms. Waverly asked.

"Um, no. I'll be fine." He gave one final guttural cough. "Here goes." Suddenly, it was as if he was in the starring role of Dr. Jekyll and Mr. Hyde. His stern expression changed to joy instantly. He should be an actor!

MY HEART

Hearts remind me of a special teacher
Her hair is the color of cobwebs
But there are no spiders living in there, I don't think…

Before Eddie could finish, the class burst into laughter. Ms. Waverly touched her hair and looked concerned as if she just now realized her hair was white. Eddie scowled and the class got instantly quiet. He still had that bully power that kids instinctively feared. He started his poem again.

MY HEART

Hearts remind me of a special teacher
Her hair is the color of cobwebs
But there are no spiders living in there, I don't think
If I could pick a special valentine,
It would be you, Ms. Waverly.

The room was eerily quiet. I saw Ms. Waverly fanning herself with her clipboard. She took a few steps back and accidentally bumped into her own desk. Her cherished glass apple went sliding across the top of her desk before it rolled onto the floor breaking into a million pieces. Bits of cherry red glass landed around Eddie's feet. Everything was happening in slow motion.

No amount of bully power stopped the class this time. A volcano of laughter erupted from the lips of every fifth grader. I saw Eddie's face go from pink to red to crimson. He hung his head and shuffled to his seat. The great and mighty Eddie finally knew what it was like to be teased.

THWAP! Ms. Waverly's ruler hit her desk. Everyone froze. That's when I noticed her face was kind of red too. I didn't know teachers could get embarrassed. "That's enough," she said with an icy edge to her voice. "Eddie, that was a lovely poem. Now, would you and Josh please go get the custodian's dust pan and broom so we can clean up this mess?" she asked.

Eddie sprinted out of the room. I had to run just to catch up with him. I saw him wipe his eyes with his hand. Was he crying?

"Hey, wait up," I called.

He slowed down and turned to face me. His eyes were red. "I bet you had a good laugh huh, Josh?" he asked.

What could I say? It was hilarious, but I didn't think he would get so upset. "Come on, Eddie. It wasn't that bad."

"Really?" he asked.

"Really. It's no worse than being crowned class farter," I added.

"How's that worse? I've won that title last year fair and square from Carter the Farter."

"I'm pretty sure I've got you beat this year."

"Yeah, you do," he laughed. "But everyone was laughing at me and now they think I have a crush on Ms. Waverly. How can I face them?"

"Gee, Eddie, it sucks to have people laugh at you doesn't it?" I said getting kind of angry. Six years of Eddie picking on me weren't going to be erased in one day.

"Yeah, you're right." And then Eddie said something I couldn't believe. "Sorry if I ever made you feel like that."

I was speechless. *Did Eddie just have a change of heart?*

"Anyway, I'll just play it off like I was goofing around. Everyone will know it was a joke."

"Do that and you lose the bet, remember? Everyone has to think you really love Ms. Waverly." I added realizing too late that I just reminded him how not to lose the bet.

"Thanks, Josh. You're real good at making someone feel better."

"Great. I'll just add that to my list of talents. Class farter and cheerer-upper."

"That's funny," was all Eddie said and laughed.

*   *   *

"So, how is everything going boys?" Ms. Behr asked.

Eddie and I rocked back and forth in our rocking chairs. I was really starting to like rocking chairs even if I didn't like the sessions with Ms. Behr.

"Okay," I mumbled. Eddie just shrugged for an answer.

"I'd like to try something different today," she said. "First, take these index cards."

She gave each of us two index cards and a clipboard and pencil.

"Josh, you need to write one thing that Eddie is really good at on the first card. And Eddie you need to do the same for Josh."

What was Eddie really good at? Burping? No, I can't put that. Farting? Ms. Behr would have a cow. Eddie wrote something quickly. That was fast. Not to be outdone, I quickly scribbled something down too.

Ms. Behr took the cards. "Now on the second card, Josh is going to write something down that he wished Eddie was better at and Eddie is going to write something he wished Josh was better at."

Eddie scribbled away again. He didn't even need a minute to think about it. It took me a little longer.

CHAPTER 13

I couldn't believe all the junk food my dad and Allie had bought for tonight. There was popcorn, soft drinks, pretzels and mini-sized candy bars. When Eddie and I asked if we could each have a friend spend the night on Saturday, our parents were really happy. Allie kept saying over and over how nice it was for Eddie to have a friend. I could tell it embarrassed him a little. Good, I thought to myself, because he asked Paul to spend the night. Paul was my friend. Not my best friend of course, that was Manny, but still my second best friend.

"Allie, I don't think we need this much food," I said as I watched Allie put it all on the counter.

"Well, maybe you don't. But I've been having a lot of cravings lately, mostly for salty and sweet food."

"Honey, they don't want to hear about your cravings," my dad said and hushed her up.

"Yeah, Mom I always crave salt and sugar. What's the big deal?" Eddie said.

Eddie and I shared a look that said parents can be so weird.

"Hey Dad, do you think we could camp out in the attic room tonight?" I asked.

"I don't see why not, the electricity is on and the plumbing is working in the new bathroom. But there's no TV hooked up yet," he answered.

"It's okay, we can tell ghost stories," Eddie said.

That did sound like fun. Wait, I had to remember this was Eddie. He'd probably try and pull some prank at my expense. Still, we could haul our mattresses upstairs and pump up the air mattresses for Paul and Manny.

"I'll order some pizzas for dinner," Allie added. "I'm sure you're both ready for something gooey and cheesy after eating so healthy this week. And I thought Josh might need a break from vegetables."

"Why?" I added even though pizza sounded great.

"I just heard you've been a bit gassy at school lately," she answered.

"You heard that?" I couldn't believe it!

My dad came to Allie's defense. "Now Josh, Ms. Behr was just giving us an update on your counseling sessions and she just happened to mention you've been gassy, that's all."

"You mean me *and* Eddie's counseling sessions. Aren't those private?"

Allie jumped back in. "Of course they are, Josh. She doesn't tell us what you talk about. She just mentioned that you and Eddie were working through some issues. It's nothing to be ashamed of. Your dad and I were going to suggest family counseling anyway, it's hard to blend two families."

"But you boys have been making real progress. Ms. Waverly said Eddie's grades are way up and now he's losing weight. And you haven't been getting picked on like before," my dad added.

"That's because Eddie was the one picking on me!" I wailed.

"I know, and now you two are friends and…"

"We are not friends," I said.

"Are you sure?" My dad winked at me.

Just then the doorbell rang.

*　　　*　　　*

Manny held the flashlight under his chin. It made his face look scary.

"And that's when my cousin's, best friend's, brother's head blew off from eating pop rocks and drinking soda at the same time. The End," Manny said.

A pillow sailed from under Paul's head and smacked Manny squarely in the face. "That was the lamest ghost story I ever heard. And it wasn't even a real ghost story, plus you told us that story at lunch last week," Paul added and Manny just shrugged.

"Do you want to hear a real scary ghost story?" I asked.

"Yeah," they all said at once.

"Okay, toss me the flashlight." Manny tossed me the flashlight. It went sailing into an arc before I caught it perfectly in my hands. We'd set up the room so our mattresses made a big plus sign on the floor. That way, we could all lie on our stomachs and have our heads facing each other. I put the flashlight under my chin and began.

"There was this guy in this room and he was the last man on earth," I started.

"Why was he the last man on earth?" Manny asked.

"It doesn't matter," I added.

"I bet it was because a virus wiped out the planet and everyone got sick and died." Paul added.

"Maybe it was aliens," Manny guessed.

"That's not possible," Eddie chimed in.

"Why not?" Manny asked.

"Aliens already landed here. I saw it on TV. I watched this show about how an alien spacecraft crashed in Roswell, New Mexico in 1947. Then the government tried to cover it up by saying it was a weather balloon."

"No way! That's cool!" Paul said.

"Yeah, what happened next?" Manny asked.

"Hello? I'm telling a ghost story here!" I interjected.

"What happened next was that the government moved the aliens and the spacecraft to a secret base called Area 51," Eddie continued as if I didn't exist.

"Wow! I thought that was all made up," Paul said in awe of Eddie and his astonishing alien facts.

"Nope, it's the truth my friend. The real truth," Eddie said nodding his head knowingly while raising one eyebrow. "And don't get me started about the moon cover-up."

"There are aliens on the moon?" Manny asked.

"Hey," I interrupted, "do you want to hear the ghost story or not?"

"I want to hear about the moon," Manny said.

Traitor. Eddie spent the next few minutes spewing off some nonsense about how we never really landed on the moon. That it was all some secret government cover-up. Meanwhile, my two friends just lapped it up.

Allie and my dad appeared at the top of the stairs with a load of extra blankets and a bowl of popcorn. Allie had her hand in the popcorn bowl and was munching away.

"Oh Eddie, you're not telling that moon story again. We did go to the moon. You can't believe everything on TV." Allie sighed and then reached for another handful of popcorn.

Eddie just shrugged and took the popcorn bowl.

"I brought up a night-light for you fellas. I know you guys aren't afraid of the dark, but this will keep you from stubbing your toe if you need to use the bathroom tonight." My dad looked at me when he said this. I could tell he was sending me a message to keep my mouth shut about Eddie's fear of the dark.

"Thanks, Dad," I said letting him know I got the message loud and clear. He gave me a smile and a nod that let me know I was a good kid. Eddie looked relieved.

"Hey Josh, weren't you in the middle of a ghost story," Eddie said as my parents left the room.

"Oh yeah," I said and continued. "There was this guy in this room and he was the last man on earth."

"Except for the aliens," Eddie said and we all burst into laughter.

Are there aliens on the moon?

CHAPTER 14

"**P**ink?" How did all of my underwear turn pink?" I cried as I looked at the underwear in my dresser drawer on Monday morning.

"Oh, yeah, about that," Eddie smirked. "It seems that a red sock got into the washing machine while Jack was doing the laundry."

"So?"

"So, the red dye in the sock turned all the white clothes pink."

"What? You did this so I couldn't win the bet. You knew I wouldn't streak across the cafetorium stage in pink underwear! You're so, so…"

"So what?"

"So diabolical," I spat.

"I know."

"Do you even know what diabolical means?" I asked.

"Um, no. But it sounds like something I'd be."

"It is." Eddie wasn't the only one who learned things from television. It meant extremely cruel or evil.

And that was Eddie, pure evil. Although, I wish I had thought of doing that to his underwear.

My dad knocked on the bedroom door and entered.

"Am I interrupting something?" he asked.

"Eddie sabotaged my underwear!" I yelled.

My dad just laughed. "A red sock accidentally got mixed up with the whites. I did the load of laundry so it must have been my fault. Looks like we will all be wearing pink underwear for a while, including me.

"Eddie doesn't seem to have any pink underwear, isn't that strange?" I said to my dad, even though I was looking straight at Eddie who paraded around the room in a very baggy pair of white underwear.

"I guess he was lucky. I'll pick up some new white ones tonight," my dad said.

"But Dad, I can't wear pink underwear. Everyone will laugh," I exclaimed.

"Josh, how will they know you're wearing pink underwear?" my dad inquired.

"Yeah, Josh, how will they know?" Eddie teased.

"I guess they won't," I said glumly.

"I thought you liked pink. Allie told me it was your favorite color," my dad added.

"It is not my favorite color!"

"Then why did you ask for a pink skateboard?"

"I didn't! Agh! Never mind. I give up."

My dad looked around our room. He noticed that our mattresses were missing. "Where may I ask are your mattresses?"

"We decided to keep them upstairs in the attic. It's really fun sleeping up there." Eddie said.

"So, you both decided to move up there," my dad said. He looked very happy.

"Um, no. We haven't decided who's moving up there, yet," I quickly said.

"We're both trying it out to see who has the better fit," Eddie said.

"I see. Well, you'd both better get dressed. The school bus will be here soon." my dad said and left the room. He didn't look as happy as before.

"Looks like I'll be winning the bet today," Eddie said.

I just stared at my top dresser drawer which was filled with row after row of perfectly folded pink underwear.

*   *   *

Eddie looked cool as a cucumber on the bus ride to school. He didn't seem worried at all about the bet. I had two very mixed emotions today. I was nervous that Eddie might actually win the bet and I was also relieved that I didn't have to run across the cafetorium stage in my underwear. Maybe I'm a coward after all.

I decided to try to make Eddie nervous so he might chicken out. Then maybe I'd have a chance to win tomorrow. Eddie was in the middle of one of his favorite gross-out stories. He truly was a first class storyteller.

"There it sat, a half-finished Snicker's bar on the table in the Teachers' Lounge. I saw it through a crack in the door. But how to get it without getting caught? And who left it on the table? What if it was a really smelly person like Nurse Turley? Then it would probably taste like chocolate, caramel, peanuts and tuna fish," Eddie said.

"Disgusting!" Marina said as the rest of us laughed.

I got so wrapped up in the story I forgot about my plan of making Eddie nervous. I found myself asking, "What happened next?"

"Well, class just started. I knew the teachers were already in the classroom. I also knew I'd get in trouble for being late to class. But I had that covered, too."

"How?" Manny asked.

"Easy, when a teacher asks why you were late, you just say you were in the bathroom going number two."

"Gross!" Marina and Chelsea said at the same time.

"Works every time. Teachers never question a number two."

"It's still gross," Chelsea said turning up her nose.

"Anyway, I ran into the Teacher's Lounge and quickly grabbed the bar. I sprinted to the boy's bathroom so I could eat it in private."

"Why do most of your stories take place in the boy's bathroom?" Marina asked.

"I think that's obvious," he answered as Marina continued to look perplexed. "Duh, because you can hide in the stalls. Just make a few grunts and everyone will leave you alone."

"So, did you ever find out who left the Snicker's bar?" I asked.

"Yes I did."

"How?" Manny asked.

"Do you really want to know?"

"Yes."

"One word: tuna fish!"

"It was Turley's!" Manny said and we all laughed.

*   *   *

I munched on a carrot stick. It was sweet and crunchy.

"You've been eating so healthy lately, Josh," Marina said as we sat at our usual lunch table.

"Yeah, Eddie's mom has been packing our lunches."

"That must be why Eddie's lost so much weight," Marina added.

Eddie blushed. He actually blushed. And then it hit me. A sure fire way to stop Eddie from running across the stage in the cafetorium today. And none too soon. I noticed him eyeballing the stage. Like he was trying to pick the best time to make his move.

"You really have lost weight, Eddie. It's like your clothes just hang on you," I said.

Eddie just grunted.

"I bet if you took your belt off, your pants would fall down," I added. That got his attention.

"Why would I take my belt off?" he asked.

"No reason. But I'd bet it would be hard to keep your underwear up."

Bull's eye! Eddie finally got it.

"Oh, crud," he said.

"That would be funny," Manny said.

"Yeah, I'd like to see that," Paul said.

"Please keep your belt on," Marina added.

I knew I was safe for one more day. Eddie wouldn't run across the cafetorium in his underwear if there was a risk that he would end up stark naked.

*   *   *

Eddie scribbled away at his homework for five solid minutes. Then after the commercials were over, he turned his attention back to the program on TV about the lost city of Atlantis.

I sat at the dining room table finishing up my math homework. My dad came home and plopped a couple of bags of brand new underwear on the table next to me.

"Here you go. Nice white underwear. No more pink for you," he said.

I felt a pit form in my stomach. I didn't have an excuse to back out now. But at least I'd have an edge over Eddie. My new tightie-whities were way better than his baggy bottoms.

My dad threw a couple of bags of underwear to Eddie, too.

"Hey, why does he get new underwear? His are still white. That's not fair." I said.

My dad gave me one of those I'm disappointed in you looks. "Well, Josh. I noticed Eddie's underwear was very loose this morning and I thought I'd buy him some that fit a little better. Is that alright with you?" he asked perturbed.

"Um, yeah I guess," I said feeling defeated.

"Cool! Thanks Jack," Eddie said.

"It's nice to hear a thank you," my dad said and looked right at me when he said it.

Great. I lost my edge now that Eddie had good fitting underwear. All thanks to my dad.

*   *   *

It was Tuesday and I was armed with my clean, new tightie-whities. I was ready for the dare. At least my body was, my mind still had many doubts. Like, if I actually go through with it, could I get suspended from school? That would go on my permanent record and I would never get into college. Or a good college, as my dad would say. My dad would definitely kill me. Ms. Waverly would definitely kill me. Principal Duff would definitely kill me and maybe even Ms. Behr. There were a lot of people who could make it difficult for me to go on to sixth grade. *Was it really worth it?*

"I'm feeling lucky today, how 'bout you, shrimpo?" Eddie said as we made our way to the cafetorium.

"Yeah, um, me too," I said but even I heard the nervousness in my voice.

"Well, you don't sound lucky."

"This is my lucky voice. You've just never heard it before," I said.

"I guess," was all he said.

The doors to the cafetorium were closed and Principal Duff was standing in front of them. He was whispering to Ms. Waverly. Even though I couldn't hear what he was saying, I knew it was something bad. Ms. Waverly was wringing her hands and kept muttering, "Oh no".

"Class, please turn around and head back to our room. We will be eating lunch in our classroom today. For those of you who didn't bring your lunch, sandwiches and milk will be sent to our room," Ms. Waverly said.

As soon as we turned around the rumors began.

"I wonder what happened?" Chelsea asked.

"Probably an oven fire. My guess is that the kitchen wasn't up to code." Marina said.

"Do you even know what that means?" Manny asked.

"No, not really, but it makes sense," Marina answered.

"I bet it was a water leak and the lunch ladies are in there swimming around trying to make sandwiches," Eddie said.

"Nothing worse than a soggy sandwich," Paul added.

Before I could contribute a scenario, we all heard the unmistakable far-off wail of an ambulance. Everyone froze. Hearing that siren could only mean one thing; something very serious happened in the cafetorium.

"Everyone, please keep moving." Ms. Waverly was practically pushing us into our room.

Once we were all back inside, Ms. Waverly closed the door. We all moved our desks into our normal lunch time cluster.

"Do you think one of the lunch ladies died?" Paul asked.

"Yeah, I hope it wasn't Miss Betty. She always gave me extra mashed potatoes." Eddie said.

"It could be Miss Yvette, she's really old. Once she told me I reminded her of her grandson. So that must make her about eighty or so," Manny said.

I wanted to add something but all I could think about was how lucky I was that the cafetorium was closed today.

"Miss Yvette has the same hair color as Ms. Waverly," Chelsea said, and then looked at Eddie. "Do you think Miss Waverly is eighty?"

All our eyes were on Eddie.

"How would I know?" He said.

"Because you seem to have a special interest in her lately," Marina said.

Everyone laughed except Eddie. Luckily for him, there was a knock on the door and the room grew quiet. His moment of getting teased was over fast. Ms. Waverly opened the door for Ms. Behr. She was carrying a huge tray full of sandwiches and small cartons of milk. Regular and chocolate. Ms. Behr placed the tray on Ms. Waverly's desk and hurried out.

"Please come up and get a sandwich and milk if you didn't bring your lunch." Ms. Waverly had to shout because the sirens were getting closer.

A few kids sauntered up to her desk. Not many kids ate the school lunch unless it was a really good menu. Today was turkey surprise which was not that popular. If this would have happened on Friday, it would have been a major crisis. Friday is always pizza day. Everyone eats school lunch that day.

"Okay, it looks like we have some milk and sandwiches left over. If anybody wants some, feel free to come up," Ms. Waverly announced.

Eddie, Paul, Manny and I all jumped up. Marina and Chelsea didn't move. I grabbed a chocolate milk. I saw Eddie swipe a couple of sandwiches. The siren was blaring and we could see the ambulance lights flashing and flickering across the room. A few kids got up to

126

look through the windows, but Ms. Waverly made them sit down.

As soon as they sat down, the siren went dead. But the lights continued to shine around the room. It was a bit eerie.

As I sipped my milk, I watched Eddie munch down on his sandwich. He could be quite the messy eater.

"Hey, Josh. I guess we weren't so lucky after all." He wiped his mouth with the back of his sleeve.

"I suppose not," I said.

Eddie raised his hand.

"Yes, Eddie?" Ms. Waverly said.

"Did you know that the word ambulance is always spelled backwards on the front of the ambulance?" He asked her.

"Yes, I did. But I bet some of your classmates didn't know that. Do you know why it is spelled backwards?"

"Yeah, it's backwards so if you're driving and you look in your rear-view mirror it looks normal. Then you can see it and get out of the way."

The class looked skeptical. "That's absolutely right, Eddie," Ms. Waverly said smiling.

We all sprung out of our seats and scurried to the windows. He was right. Eddie was right! In big, bold letters the word **AMBULANCE** was splashed across the front of the ambulance.

A crowd was forming around Eddie and I could hear comments like; awesome, cool and he's right! My guess was that he watched a show on television about emergency transport vehicles.

But before Eddie could dazzle the crowd with more information, we all saw Miss Betty on a stretcher.

She was being wheeled into the back of the ambulance. Her leg looked crooked and a make-shift splint had been placed around it.

"Oh no, not Miss Betty," Eddie said.

"Well, at least she's alive," Paul said.

"That's good," Manny said.

"Yeah, but no more extra potatoes," Eddie said sadly. "I guess it wasn't her lucky day either, huh, Josh?"

"I guess not," I said, but it sure turned out to be mine. I was safe for another day.

CHAPTER 15

Weird flashes of light bounced around the attic room early Wednesday morning. I looked at my alarm clock. I still had thirty minutes left to sleep. I peered over at Eddie's mattress. It was empty except for piles of sheets and blankets all wrapped up in a heap. *How does he sleep in that mess?* Another flash of light and then I heard the soft tapping of a hammer. I raced to the light switch and in a moment the room was flooded in brightness.

There stood Eddie, in his pajamas, balancing on a chair that was propped up against the wall. He was holding a small hammer in one hand and the end of his eagle poster in the other. In his mouth was a small flashlight. That explained the weird flashes.

"Dang, Josh. You almost made me fall." He continued to nail the last corner of the poster to the wall. TAP, TAP, TAP, went the miniature hammer.

"What are you doing?" I asked, rubbing the sleep from my eyes. I couldn't believe Eddie was so awake. I usually had to shake him up every morning. And there he was, bright-eyed and bushy-tailed as my dad would say, decorating the attic with more of his stuff.

"What's it look like I'm doing? I'm hanging up my poster."

"It's not your room yet," I said.

"It's not yours either but that didn't stop you from hanging up those stupid math flash card things on the wall next to your desk."

"Those are for studying." I had my dad help me move my desk up yesterday. I told him it was quieter for studying up in the attic. I don't think he believed me. And then he helped Eddie move his desk up, too. No fair.

"Well, this eagle poster helps me study."

I surveyed my surroundings. It just dawned on me that both Eddie and I had been secretly hauling all our stuff upstairs. The only stuff left in our old room were our dressers, nightstands and the bunk-bed frame. The attic appeared very lived in already. Eddie's games, music and electronics were scattered all over the place and my books were all perfectly stacked and in alphabetical order. I hated to admit it but the last couple of nights we'd been playing video games against each other before lights out and it was fun. I even won a couple of times.

My thoughts went back to Eddie and his poster, which did look great on the wall. "Why are you up so early, couldn't this have waited 'til after school?"

"I'm so glad you asked, Josh. I couldn't wait because today is the day I win the bet. I wanted to get an early start on what will forever be known as Eddie's Attic Triumph or E.A.T., if you will," he boasted.

"You do know that spells eat, right?"

"Oh, I might have to rethink that. Anyway, I really didn't mean to wake you, but since you're up, could you give me a hand with my nightstand. I'd like to get it in place this morning. It's too heavy to move by myself, I've already tried."

"Okay, but we have to move mine too, because I'm going to win today," I said.

"Fine, we'll bring them both up but after school one of them will be going right back down the stairs."

"Fine," I said.

"Double fine," he replied.

*   *   *

The entire cafetorium was buzzing with chatter except for our table.

"You're awfully quiet today," Marina said to Eddie.

"Yeah, did you finally run out of stories?" Manny asked.

Eddie ignored them. Only I knew why he was so quiet. He was devising his plan to run practically naked across the stage in a matter of minutes. Part of me hoped he wouldn't go through with it but I saw the determination on his face and knew he would. It was me who couldn't go through with it. Not yet, anyway. But I wasn't ready for Eddie to win yet. I needed a plan to stop him. And it had to be fool-proof.

"Hey, Josh. Want my chocolate milk?" Paul asked.

That's it! Chocolate milk. It was so easy. I can't believe I didn't think of it sooner.

"Um, sure," I said. I caught the milk that Paul hurled at me with one hand. Marina and Chelsea looked impressed. To bad Eddie missed it, he would have approved. He was still off in his own world and hadn't yet contributed to our lunchtime banter.

"Thanks," I said.

Time to put my plan into motion. All I had to do was wait for Eddie to make his move. And as if reading my mind, Eddie came back to life bringing with him a bright spark to our dull group.

"And by the way," Eddie started as if he'd been part of the conversation all along, "No, I haven't run out of stories. I have billions. As a matter of fact, in a few moments you will witness the birth of a new legend. This story is about the bravest student that ever walked the halls of this elementary school."

All eyes were glued on Eddie. I tried to act as normal as I could while I carefully opened my carton of chocolate milk.

"Who?" Paul asked.

"Just be patient," Eddie said as he slid his lunch to the center of the table and slowly pushed back his chair.

It was time. Eddie was getting ready to leave us. He looked at the stage. Here he would find his glory and the school would witness a new era of bravado. It was now or never.

I started making several, fake, puny sneezes that led to beefier and louder sneezes. All the eyes that were focused on Eddie shifted in my direction. I had to make them all believe I was having a sneezing attack for my plan to work.

"Are you okay?" Marina asked concerned.

"Maybe you should drink some water," Chelsea added.

"He doesn't have the hiccups, he has the sneezes. Water won't work," Manny said.

Good. My plan was working. They believed me. Now for the finale! A sneeze that would blow away all of the sneezes in the world.

"AH, AH, AH, CHOOOOO!!!"

As I overacted my award-winning sneeze I violently thrust my body sideways, spilling my entire carton of chocolate milk right into Eddie's lap. Gooey, chocolaty goodness sloshed between Eddie's legs and pooled around his bottom. I did it!

Eddie jumped up like his pants were on fire. Now everyone could see the muddy-brown stains across the front and back of his pants. "Josh, you did that on purpose!"

"No, I didn't. I was having a sneezing attack. Thank you very much," I said.

"You sure do seem okay now," he said through clenched teeth.

"Yeah, I just needed to get it out of my system," I told him.

"Is everything alright here?" Mr. Duff asked as he made his way to our table.

"Um, Josh had a sneezing attack and accidentally spilled his milk on Eddie," Marina said softly.

Mr. Duff looked at Eddie and then at Eddie's pants. "Is that right, Eddie? Was it an accident?"

Eddie calmed himself down and said, "Yeah, just an accident."

"Okay, would you like to go to my office and call your mom to bring you new pants?" Mr. Duff asked Eddie.

"Naw, I'll be alright. They'll dry in a while. Thanks," Eddie said.

"Okay, then. Josh, please be more careful when you sneeze," Mr. Duff said looking straight at me. I could tell he didn't think it was an accident.

"Sure thing, Mr. Duff, I'll try," I mumbled.

Eddie grabbed another chair since his was still sticky from the milk. He leaned close to me and whispered, "Nice going. I can't run across the stage now. It will look like I pooped my pants because of the chocolate stains. But don't worry; I will be ready for you tomorrow. Nothing will stop me, that room is mine."

I actually felt a shiver go down my spine. I scooted away from Eddie.

"So, did I ever tell you guys about the time I got lost in a pet store and a ferret helped me find my way out?" Eddie was back to his storytelling like nothing had happened.

*   *   *

Eddie slurped his cereal at breakfast on Thursday morning. *How could he eat?* I was so nervous, I could barely force down a little oatmeal.

"This is the day," he said in between spoonfuls of milk and Cheerios.

We heard the bus pull up. Eddie sprinted for the door grabbing his backpack and jacket in one quick motion. I fumbled for mine and wished I was as coordinated as Eddie.

Eddie was his usual self all the way to school. Completely at ease and telling gross-out stories all the way there. I felt like I was going to vomit.

When I walked into the classroom, Ms. Waverly looked at me and furrowed her brow. "Is everything alright, Josh?" she asked. "You look a bit pale."

"I'm fine," I mumbled and could tell she wasn't convinced.

All through the morning, my stomach grew queasier and queasier. I even burped a little throw-up in my mouth. I knew it was just nerves, but I couldn't help it.

Eddie sat at his desk, staring off into space. Every once in a while he would solve a math problem on his worksheet. He seemed super relaxed.

As we were getting ready to line up for lunch, Ms. Behr popped into the room.

"Ms. Waverly, I have a special treat for Josh and Eddie today. I thought since they missed their session with me yesterday due to a meeting I had, that I would invite them to eat lunch with me today in my office."

"What?" Eddie said a little too loud. Ms. Behr took it to mean he was excited for the privilege of eating lunch with her. Little did she know what we had planned to do in the cafetorium today.

My stomach felt better instantly. In fact, I was kind of hungry. Eddie looked beaten.

"Come on, boys. Grab your lunches and we'll have a nice long chat," she said as we followed her out the door.

*   *   *

Ms. Behr moved a small table in the middle of the rocking chairs for our lunches. She nibbled on a turkey sandwich and potato chips. Eddie and I had our usual sandwiches and carrot sticks. Ms Behr wiped her mouth with a napkin and began packing up her lunch.

"Ms Behr, I have a very important question to ask you. I hope it's not too personal," Eddie said.

Pure delight washed over Ms. Behr's face. Maybe she thought Eddie was about to have a breakthrough. "Please, ask you question," she said with great enthusiasm.

"Well, I was just wondering…" Eddie trailed off.

"This is a safe place Eddie. You can ask whatever you want."

"Are you going to finish those chips? If not, I wouldn't mind having a few," Eddie said.

"Oh," she said and looked disappointed. "Help yourself."

Eddie munched happily on the chips.

"Now, boys I have something very important to share with you," she said and pulled out the index cards we'd filled out last Friday. "I noticed something very interesting about these cards. Let me share them with you. Or better yet, how about you share them with each other."

She handed each of us a card face down and told us not to turn it over until she said so.

"Josh, in your hand you hold the card that Eddie filled out when I asked him what he really liked about you. Eddie, you have the card Josh filled with the same question. Josh, can you tell me what Eddie wrote about you?" she asked.

I turned the card over and read it aloud, "Josh is good at making friends." I smiled at Eddie. He just nodded.

"Now it's your turn, Eddie." Ms. Behr said.

Eddie turned his card over and said, "Eddie is good at sports." He grinned. "Hey, that's true, I am good at sports."

"Now let me give you boys the other two cards. These are the cards where you wrote what you wished each other was better at." She handed us each the other card. "Eddie, read your card first this time. What did Josh write about you?"

Eddie turned the card over. "I wish Eddie was better at making friends." Eddie looked surprised. "That's weird!"

"You think that's weird, let Josh read his card. Go ahead Josh. Find out what Eddie wishes you were better at."

I turned my card over and read, "I wish Josh was better at sports. That's freaky!"

"It seems you boys know each other much better than you thought. What can you do with this information you have learned?" she asked.

"I know," Eddie said. "I could coach Josh and give him some pointers on how to be better in sports. Then we could play together more. I always wanted to play with him. Ever since kindergarten, but he never seemed interested."

"What?" I cried. "You've been picking on me since kindergarten."

"Because you never wanted to play with me. You were the kid all the other kids liked. And you were nice to everyone. Except me," he added and looked sad.

"That's crazy. You were mean to me from the first day!"

"No, I wasn't. I remember the first day of kindergarten I asked you to share the blocks with me so we could play together. You said you were building a tower and needed all the blocks for yourself. So see, you started it."

"You knocked the blocks over! How is that being a good friend?"

"I thought if I knocked them over, we could rebuild the tower together."

I sat quietly for a minute. For some reason, Eddie's dad kept popping up into my brain. I remembered how rough he was with me that one time I met him. Maybe Eddie's dad taught him to be rough instead of nice. Maybe that's why he had a hard time making friends. Until now. Eddie had friends now. He had my friends. Before I could tell him off for stealing my friends, Eddie interrupted.

"Anyway, it doesn't matter. I have lots of friends. Josh shared his friends with me. That was pretty cool."

I couldn't say anything now because I would look like a real jerk. I really didn't mind sharing my friends with Eddie anymore, if I really thought about it..

"I have some exciting news for you boys," Ms. Behr said. "This is your last counseling session with me. I am very proud of you both. You've made great progress."

Eddie beamed with pride. I smiled, too. Ms. Behr's counseling not only helped me see Eddie in a new light, but helped me see myself in a new light, too. My eyes began to water. Stupid air freshener. Ms. Behr gave us each a hug and scooted us out the door. It was then I noticed her plug-in air freshener was missing. Oh well, my dad says guys can cry too.

Eddie's and Josh's Index Cards

CHAPTER 16

Eddie unwrapped the present quickly. Wrapping paper went flying everywhere. I took my time. I liked to savor the anticipation of what the gift might be.

"Wow! A new art set. This is awesome!" Eddie yelled and hugged Allie and my dad.

It was a really nice art set. Lots of paint, brushes, a sketchbook, and some markers. I continued to unwrap my gift. The corner showed through and I saw beautifully colored paper. The sheets were all shiny and full of decoration. With that I unwrapped the entire gift. There was also a book and the title was: *A Beginners Guide to Origami*. It had a really cool cover that showed a bunch of animals made out of folded paper.

"Do you like it Josh?" Allie asked. "It's an origami book. Origami is the Japanese art of paper folding. I thought you might like it because you have to be very precise and mathematical to make it look just right."

"It looks like a lot of fun. Thanks," I answered.

Allie dabbed her eyes. She was crying. My dad just chuckled and said, "Don't worry it comes along with the territory."

I had no clue what he was talking about and didn't really care. I couldn't wait to try origami.

"We wanted to give you boys something special. Ms. Behr called today and said you were done with your counseling sessions," my dad grinned.

"I'm so proud of both of you," Allie said and burst into huge sobs. My dad chuckled again. Grown-ups can be so strange.

*   *   *

Eddie lounged on his mattress in the attic and drew in his sketchbook. I read my origami book and tried to figure out how to create a dog's head. I was getting the hang of it. The origami paper was really cool. It was perfectly square and some of it even had animal print designs on it. For the dog's head I chose a piece of white paper with black spots. It looked like a Dalmatian.

"Tomorrow's the big day," Eddie said.

I felt a pit in my stomach instantly.

"Are you ready?"

"Yeah," I mumbled.

"You don't sound ready."

"What's ready sound like?" I asked getting annoyed. I just wanted to make my Dalmatian.

"Touchy, touchy. Well, I'm ready. I was ready Wednesday, too. I would have gone through with it if you hadn't spilled chocolate milk on me."

I knew he spoke the truth. Eddie was fearless. The only reason he didn't run through the cafetorium was because his underwear was soaked with chocolate milk. I would never muster up enough courage to beat him fair and square. I had an idea.

"Hey, Eddie can I borrow your brown marker to color in my Dalmatian's eyes?"

Eddie tossed me the marker without comment. I colored in the eyes and then grabbed my stomach.

"I think I need to use the bathroom," I said as I slipped the marker up my pajama sleeve.

"Why don't you tell the world," Eddie said sarcastically.

I went to go down the stairs.

"Where are you going?" Eddie asked.

"I just said I have to go to the bathroom."

"We have a bathroom up here."

Eddie was right. I had to think fast. "Yeah, but I really have to go," I said.

"So?"

"So I might smell the place up."

"So?"

"Do you want me to smell the place up?" I asked him.

"No. But don't expect me to do the same for you. When I gotta go, I'm using our new bathroom. Deal with it."

I walked downstairs, passed by the bathroom and entered our old bedroom. I opened Eddie's underwear drawer and did something horrible and clever. Using Eddie's new brown marker, I colored a big skid-mark on the outside of each pair of his underwear. Now he would be too embarrassed to streak across the stage in his underwear. And it would be too late to get a new pair before tomorrow. It was mean, but I was playing for keeps.

The next morning I jumped out of bed. Well, off my mattress on the floor anyway and headed downstairs to get dressed. I knew I'd won the bet. Eddie would never streak with a skid-mark, no matter how brave he was.

I strolled into my old room and there was Eddie frantically pulling out all his underwear and checking them for skid-marks. He threw them on the floor and turned to me.

"What did you do?" he said and looked very angry.

"What are you talking about?" I asked innocently.

"You know darn well what I'm talking about. All the brown marks on my underwear."

"Maybe you should be more careful after using the bathroom."

"I'll pound you!" Eddie yelled.

It had been a while since Eddie had threatened me. He really could be scary when he wanted to be. I realized too late I had pushed him too far. I braced myself for the beating that was about to start.

Eddie burst into laughter. "I really had you going! You should have seen your face. You really thought I was going to pound you."

What was going on? Eddie had been pretending to be mad. *But why?*

"You really are an amateur, Josh. I gotta admit, Wednesday was brilliant with the chocolate milk, but did you think I would let it happen again?"

I just stared at him, dumbfounded.

Eddie strolled over to my dresser and opened my underwear drawer. He reached all the way in the back and pulled out a pristine pair of underwear, just his size.

"I hid this pair in there after school on Wednesday. I had a feeling you might try to sabotage my new underwear. Pretty clever huh? Hiding it in your drawer. You never suspected it, did you?"

"No," I stammered.

"Yep, clever like a prairie dog," he said and strutted to the bathroom to get dressed.

*   *   *

Not many fifth graders were willing to run through the cafetorium in just their underwear, but I had too much at stake to back out now. Here I was hiding behind the stage curtain during lunch in nothing but my tightie-whities and sneakers. I had goose bumps on my arms and legs because of our school's brand new air conditioning system. Or maybe it because I was nervous. If my dad could see me right now, he would shake his head and say, "Joshua Allen Miller, have you lost your mind? Is this any way for a eleven-year old to act?" Allie would probably cry. She'd been doing that a lot lately.

I peeked from behind the curtain and I watched my classmates wolfing down their food. The smell of pepperoni pizza filled my nostrils and made me want to puke. Normally, I enjoyed pizza, but this day was anything but normal.

Eddie stood right next to me, grinning from ear to ear. "I'm gonna go!" he challenged.

How did it get this far? A minute ago, we were eating pizza and then Eddie asked if he could use the bathroom. I knew he was making a run for it.

I asked to use the bathroom, too. I wasn't going to let him win that easily. I snuck onto the stage using the back door and stripped off everything but my underwear and my shoes. Eddie was already there, in his underwear.

The fourth graders were just entering. I put my hands over my ears to muffle out the chatter of a million different conversations going on at once. I never realized how loud it could be in the school cafetorium. No wonder it took so long for everyone to get quiet during assemblies.

I couldn't back out now. This was the third and final dare. The Ultimate Dare! I was proud of myself for getting this far.

"It's kinda cold up here, huh Josh?" Eddie asked and laughed nervously.

Was he stalling? Did Eddie, the former school bully, have cold feet?

We were safely hidden behind the curtain wing. Maybe I could talk Eddie out of doing this. He didn't seem as sure of himself as he had a minute ago.

"What are you waiting for?" I asked and inhaled deeply to calm my nerves. I instantly smelled smoke.

"Hey Josh, do you smell smoke?" he asked.

Before I could answer, the fire alarm went off. Eddie and I looked at each other in complete and total panic.

All the kids were being scooted out the doors to safety. Eddie and I started to grab our clothes, but we were stopped by the sudden appearance of Nurse Turley.

"What are you boys doing up here in your underwear?" she yelled. "We need to get out, now!" She grabbed us each by the arm and scooted us off the stage. She was a lot stronger than she looked.

"But my clothes," I said as I was pushed farther and farther away from them.

"There's no time for nonsense!" Nurse Turley yelled and added, "You should have thought of that before you stripped down to your skivvies!"

Eddie grabbed a lunch tray and held it over his underwear. Taking his cue, I grabbed the first thing I saw and did the same.

Nurse Turley practically shoved us out the exit doors. The entire school was lined up on the blacktop and unfortunately they were facing the doors as we exited. Never in my life have I felt so embarrassed. This even topped the machine gun fart episode on the bus.

At first, I thought I heard a clap of thunder. I looked up for a lightening bolt but realized the thunder-clap was really the sound of every child in the school laughing at the same time.

I turned to look at Eddie. He was laughing, too.

"Nice lunchbox," he said and pointed.

I looked down and noticed I had grabbed a pink Barbie lunchbox to cover my underwear. I looked at Eddie. The tray he had grabbed to cover his under-wear must of still had food on it. Applesauce and greenbeans covered his legs.

And then it happened. I couldn't help it. I laughed. A huge, magnificent belly laugh. And no matter how many dirty looks the teachers and principal gave me, I couldn't stop laughing.

Pan-de-mo-nium! There weren't many times when you could see the meaning of a spelling word in action. But this was one of them. We learned the meaning of pandemonium this week. It meant total chaos.

And that was exactly what was happening right now in Mr. Duff's office. Besides me and Eddie, there were my dad, Allie, Mr. Duff, Ms. Waverly and Ms. Behr. Words and accusations were flying around the room like bats on Halloween. Everyone was talking at once and the only word that I heard loud and clear was suspension. Eddie heard it too.

"Maybe we went too far," he whispered to me. I shook my head yes.

Seeing that this meeting was going nowhere fast, Mr. Duff told everyone to quiet down. "Now boys, why were you two hiding on the stage in your underwear?"

Five sets of eyes stared at us. Neither of us had the guts to talk first.

"Well?" Mr. Duff waited.

Eddie glanced at the door. I guess he was plotting his escape route.

"Josh, answer Mr. Duff," my dad said impatiently.

"Well, um, it's hard to explain but, um..."

Eddie said, "It's actually a very funny story."

"Eddie, not now. This isn't a laughing matter, it's very serious," Allie said and quietly started to cry. "I need to sit down, I think I'm going to faint."

My dad rushed to Allie's side and helped her into a chair. Ms. Behr gave her a glass of water and Ms. Waverly handed her a bunch of tissues.

"I'm fine now," Allie said. "Continue, please." She was still crying a bit.

"What Eddie meant to say was it started out funny but it didn't end that way," I said.

"Yeah, that's what I meant. It all started when you told us that one of us could move into the attic. We both wanted that room for ourselves and we didn't know how else to be fair about who got it, you see."

"I'm confused, this is about a room?" Mr. Duff asked.

My dad explained, "Allie and I told the boys they could decide who got the attic room. But without fighting, remember?"

"We didn't fight, we just came up with our own way," I said.

"And what was that?" Ms. Behr butted in.

"A series of dares," Eddie mumbled.

"What?" Allie asked.

"He said a series of dares," I repeated.

"That explains a lot," Ms. Waverly said.

Allie stopped crying. "What kind of dares?"

While Eddie and I recited the list of dares, the expressions on each attentive face was as different as the seven dwarfs. Ms. Behr looked relieved, Ms. Waverly looked embarrassed, Mr. Duff looked disappointed and my dad looked mad. Only Allie's expression didn't make sense. She went from shocked, to impressed, to upset then hysterical with laughter. I thought Eddie had a funny laugh but Allie's was out of control.

"Honey, like you said this isn't a laughing matter," my dad said to Allie. Allie tried to stop laughing but couldn't.

"Really, Mrs. Miller, these boys are suspended and need to be taken off the school property immediately," Mr. Duff said.

That stopped her laughing. "I know, I know. I'm very hormonal lately. I can't stop crying or laughing. But I do know one thing. These boys are going to make very interesting big brothers to their new little sister."

Now it was time for Eddie and me to be shocked. *Did I just hear right?*

"Mom, you're..."

"Yes. I'm pregnant. You and Josh are going to have a little sister. Believe me, this was not the way we intended to tell you." We both hugged Allie. Ms. Waverly and Ms. Behr were offering congratulations and Mr. Duff concluded the meeting was over.

As we were leaving Ms. Behr's office, my dad said to Eddie and me, "This doesn't get you boys off the hook. You're both still in big trouble and this suspension will probably go in your permanent files."

It was hard to care about permanent files and suspension with news this big. We passed a group of girls playing jump rope on our way to the car. They were singing a new song:

Nice, thin, Eddie, gave up spaghetti
Gave us treats, through old Miss Betty
Doesn't weigh a ton-ie, we keep our money
How many girls now think he's funny?
1...2...3...4...5...

"Not bad," I said to Eddie.

"Yeah, never underestimate the power of ice cream," he said.

CHAPTER 17

Eddie and I looked around the attic room. It was awesome. Our parents had moved our dressers up and where our mattresses used to be stood two sets of bunk beds. Enough for me, Eddie, Manny and Paul to each have our own bed during sleepovers. Of course, that wasn't going to happen any time soon. Our parents had even hooked up the computer.

"We had planned to surprise you with the finished room tonight, but you boys blew it," my dad said as he started unhooking the video game controller from the TV.

Allie stood and watched my dad with a sad expression on her face. "I really thought you boys were getting along. To find out it was all some stupid bet…" she trailed off.

My dad took the video game controller downstairs. He came back for the TV. Next, he took the computer. This was bad.

"Allie and I talked about a lot of different punishments for you two. At first we considered making you stay in your old room, but we realized that wouldn't be fair to us or the new baby. We need to be close to the baby for feeding and changing the diapers and we certainly don't want to walk up a flight of stairs every time the baby needs us."

"We decided, since the room meant so much to you both, then you could have it. But it would just be a plain room. A place to sleep, that's all. All of the fun and cool things that made this room special are gone," Allie added.

"Will they ever come back?" Eddie asked.

"That depends on you two. We will just have to wait and see. Maybe someday, some of the items will trickle back in or maybe they'll end up at Goodwill," she answered.

Eddie and I said nothing. We knew we didn't have a leg to stand on. The only thing left in our room besides our furniture were our books and school supplies.

"Well boys, enjoy your new room. You're going to be spending quite a lot of time up here. I'd say about a month should do for your grounding," my dad said as he and Allie left.

"A month?" Eddie said.

"What'd you expect?" I answered.

"What'd you expect, you little wiener?" Eddie said and threw me on the ground. He began gulping air. It was just like it had always been. Eddie was still a bully. Well, I had had enough. I began gulping air, too.

We both burped into each other's face, long and hard. Then we rolled on the floor laughing. I guess things were different than they had been. Eddie was my friend. My true friend. And he was my brother, too. It stank that all the fun things were gone from the room.

But the one fun thing Allie and my dad couldn't take away from me was Eddie.

"We really did blow it, didn't we Eddie?" I asked.

"Yeah, I feel really bad. Jack hates me and I made my mom cry."

"My dad doesn't hate you. He's just disappointed in you. In us."

"It's weird we're gonna have a baby sister," he said after a moment.

"You can teach her how to burp," I said.

"So could you. You're getting good. I'm pretty sure I smelled pepperoni pizza on that last one."

"Yeah, that's what I had for lunch."

"Duh, I was there. Remember the fire alarm?"

"Classic. How could I ever forget that? I can't believe it was just burned popcorn from the teacher's lounge."

"I know. We will forever be legends at our school. No one will ever top us."

"Our story will live on forever," I added. "Someday, many years from now of course, kids will still tell the amazing tale of The Underwear Dare!"

"We'll be living legends like the Swamp Ape or the Loch Ness Monster," he said.

"Except we'll be real," I added.

"What do you mean? The Swamp Ape and the Loch Ness Monster are real," he said.

*   *   *

"Get up, boys. You've got a lot of work to do," my dad announced the next morning. "Since you lost your TV and computer privileges, you both have a lot of free time. I figured you two could start by raking the yard."

I had a feeling this was going to be a long month. Eddie and I spent most of the morning raking leaves into a big pile.

"Hey Josh, check this out," Eddie said and fell over backwards into the huge pile of leaves.

"Let me try!" I said.

"Wait, let me pretend to shoot you."

"Okay."

Eddie did his best gangster imitation, "Alright you dirty rat. This is the end of the line for you."

Eddie really sounded like an old time gangster. He was a pretty good actor.

"Bang!" he yelled.

I flung myself backward into the pile of leaves. They felt soft and crunched loudly. They smelled all earthy like plants and soil.

"My turn! You shoot me," Eddie yelled.

"Alright, mister," I said even though my gangster imitation sucked compared to Eddie's. "It's over for you. Bang!"

Eddie flew backwards. It really looked like he had been shot. He sat up in the pile of leaves and laughed. Just then my dad came out with a hand full of garbage bags.

"Looks like you're ready to bag up the leaves," he said putting an end to our fun.

*   *   *

Eddie and I spent the rest of the afternoon in our room. Eddie wandered around in circles. I could tell he was bored.

"I miss TV," he said.

"I know and it's only been half a day."

"I miss the internet."

"Me too."

"What can we do?" Eddie said as he rummaged through the closet. "What do we have here?" he asked as he pulled out his sketchbook.

"Hey, I put my origami stuff in there, too!" I scrambled to get it.

Eddie and I began to create art.

"My mom was still really mad today," Eddie said.

"She seemed a bit better."

"Naw, she's mad. I could tell because she didn't make a special breakfast. Saturday's breakfast is always big and delicious. Today she just gave us cold cereal."

"Maybe she has morning sickness. I heard pregnant ladies can get sick in the morning."

"That's stupid. It can't be true."

Eddie continued to draw and after a while he said, "We should do something nice for my mom."

"Like what?"

"I dunno, you're the one with the brains. You think of something."

"We could help around the house."

"Boring."

"Sometimes you have to do things that are boring if you want to help people."

"Yeah, but what if we did something less boring. Less boring things can help, too."

"You think of it then."

"We could make her a card," Eddie said.

"That's for babies," I said.

"That's it. You are smart."

"What's it?" I asked.

"We could make something for the baby. We've got everything we need here to do it."

"Let's do it," I said enthusiastically.

Eddie and I spent the rest of the day creating art for the baby. I got really good at making origami animals. Eddie decided to paint animals. Together we created an art zoo.

Eddie made a really cool painting of an elephant in the jungle. I taught myself how to fold a penguin and bear out of origami paper. I used Eddie's markers to add eyes and noses to the animals.

Next, Eddie painted a monkey swinging from a tree. The cool thing was, when it was next to the elephant painting, it looked like it was the same scene. He somehow made the jungle match up between the paintings.

I taught myself how to fold a pig, a swan and a frog. Then I made about ten more copies of each animal.

"You're getting good at origami," Eddie said.

"Thanks. Your paintings look great. I like how they look like one scene."

"Check this out," Eddie said and added his final painting to the line up. It was a giraffe. He had painted it so its head was up in the tree looking at the monkey. He was a gifted artist.

"It's really good," I said.

"Thanks," he answered and I could tell he was proud.

"What should I do with all these origami animals?" I asked.

"You could string them together and we could hang them in the baby's room."

"Along with your paintings."

"It'll look great."

Later that night when Allie and my dad were asleep, Eddie and I snuck downstairs to secretly decorate the baby's room with our creations. For once Eddie's feet didn't sound like a caveman's feet clomping down the stairs.

Eddie snuck some yarn out of Allie's knitting basket and we tied the origami animals to the long yarn. We hung up Eddie's paintings using old thumbtacks from our bulletin board and we strung the origami animals across the room.

It felt good to do something nice for Allie. And Eddie was right, it wasn't boring.

CHAPTER 18

Sausage. Yummy breakfast sausage. I jumped out of bed and rushed downstairs. I bumped into Eddie on the way.

"Out of my way, shrimpo," Eddie yelled and passed me on the stairs. This time I didn't care. I knew there would be enough sausage to go around.

Allie put a heaping plate of pancakes and sausage in front of me, Eddie, and my dad. I poured warm maple syrup over my plateful and dug in.

Allie joined us at the table.

"I want to thank you boys for the beautiful art in the baby's room. I'm sure you did it out of the goodness of your heart. It's not a bribe, is it?" Allie asked.

"We felt really bad for upsetting you and Jack. We were trying to show you we were sorry," Eddie said.

"We really are sorry," I added sounding like a parrot.

My dad looked over his glasses at Allie. "Well, saying you're sorry is a good place to start but that doesn't make up for what you two did. You can think about it this afternoon in your room. It's raining too hard for yard work. And you both will load the dishwasher when you're done with breakfast."

We ate the rest of our breakfast in silence and then loaded the dishwasher. We trudged up the stairs to our room and plopped on our beds.

"Check this out," Eddie said as he picked up a deck of cards off his nightstand.

"Where'd those come from?" I asked.

"My mom. They're the same deck that my mom, dad, and I used to play with. She must have put them up here while we were loading the dishwasher."

"I guess she's not as mad as before," I said.

"You want to play Hearts?"

"I don't know how."

"I'll teach you, but it's kinda hard to play with just two people."

"Okay," I said as he dealt the first hand and explained the rules. After we'd been playing awhile I said, "Do you think our parents will let us name our sister?"

"Probably. If we convince them we want to be a part of it all."

"We should pick a really cool name."

"Like Alwilda," Eddie said.

"What? That stinks."

"No it doesn't. If you know your history then you know Alwilda was a princess."

"So, there were lots of princesses in history."

"Not like Alwilda. She was the princess of Scandinavia or something and she was supposed to marry Prince Alf of Denmark."

"Alf? Sounds stupid, like a muppet."

"Whatever. Anyway, she thought Prince Alf was a wimp so she dressed up like a man and became a pirate and sailed away."

"So that's it?"

"Ah, no that's not it. Her pirate ship got into a battle with Prince Alf's ship. He won and took her prisoner. She was so impressed by his unwimpiness that she married him and became the Queen of Denmark."

"Cool. But Alwilda is still an ugly name. What would her nickname be, Al? If you want a stupid pirate name why not name her Scurvy. That's just as bad."

"Duh, Josh. Scurvy is a good name for a dog, but not a person. Everyone knows that. So, what's your choice?"

"I was thinking Hannah."

"What? There are a million girls named Hannah."

"Yeah, but Hannah is a palindrome," I added.

"What's a palindrome? I could get on board with the name Palindrome. That's a cool name."

"Palindrome is not a name. It's when a word is spelled the same forward and backward. Like tot, T-O-T."

"Yum, tater tots. Are we having those for lunch? Wait! I get it. Like poop. P-O-O-P forwards or backwards it's P-O-O-P. That's awesome!" Eddie said.

"So you agree, Hannah is cool," I said.

"I do agree Hannah is cool. I like Palindrome better, but Alwilda is the best. And I'm willing to bet on it. Do you care to bet on it?" Eddie goaded me.

"Yes, I am willing to make a bet on it. The winner gets to name our sister. What kind of bet?" I asked.

Eddie smiled slyly and said, "I'm thinking about a series of dares…"

ABOUT THE AUTHORS

This book was written by the Nardini Sisters. Lisa Nardini lives in Florida and Gina Nardini-Christoffel lives in North Carolina. Although the two sisters live in different states, they still make time to write together. While growing up in the Ozarks, they shared a bedroom and according to Gina, Lisa got all the good wall space and shelves.

The Underwear Dare is their first novel. They are currently working on *The Field Trip* which features the same cast of characters from *The Underwear Dare* as they venture into sixth grade.

Visit their website at:
www.nardinisisters.com

Made in the USA
Lexington, KY
29 September 2012